BECAUSE WE BELIEVED
A CHRISTIAN ROMANCE

JULIETTE DUNCAN

TRANSFORMED BY LOVE SERIES - BOOK 4

Cover Design by http://www.StunningBookCovers.com

Copyright © 2020 Juliette Duncan

All rights reserved.

BECAUSE WE BELIEVED is a work of fiction. Names, characters, and incidents are all products of the author's imagination or are used for fictional purposes. Any mentioned brand names, places, and trade marks remain the property of their respective owners, bear no association with the author, and are used for fictional purposes only.

THE HOLY BIBLE, NEW INTERNATIONAL VERSION®, NIV® Copyright © 1973, 1978, 1984, 2011 by Biblica, Inc.™ Used by permission. All rights reserved worldwide.

PRAISE FOR "BECAUSE WE BELIEVED"

"This was a tearjerker but also filled with hope for those in abusive situations. The talks Marta gives are talks I hope those that read this book will also encourage their daughters to read. Hopefully & prayerfully forewarned can be a deterrent to wrong relationships." ~*Patricia*

"Loved it! This was a great, clean read. I loved the action and danger in it. I also loved the religious aspect. Not too much to where you feel it's preachy, but just right, to make you think. Definitely worth the read!" ~*Teresa*

"This is a book that is full of emotions. It hooks you on the first page and doesn't let go. It's a wonderful inspirational story about overcoming your past and helping others who are struggling." ~*Ann*

"This is an amazing book full of emotion and inspiration." ~*Barb*

FOREWORD

HELLO! Thank you for choosing to read this book - I hope you enjoy it! Please note that this story is set in Australia. Australian spelling and terminology have been used and are not typos!

As a thank you for reading this book, I'd like to offer you a FREE GIFT. That's right - my FREE novella, "Hank and Sarah - A Love Story" is available exclusively to my newsletter subscribers. Click here to claim your copy now and to be notified of my future book releases. I hope you enjoy both books! Have a wonderful day!

Juliette

CHAPTER 1

Paul Peterson, the new chaplain at Salford Christian School, glanced at the clock for the third time in less than a minute as he waited for Marta Rodriguez to arrive for their appointment. These types of conversations were never easy, and he especially wasn't looking forward to this one.

It wasn't so much that Angel, the woman's six-year-old daughter, was being bullied. More that the incessant questioning by the other children was clearly distressing the little girl, and her mother needed to know. But it was a sensitive subject and he didn't quite know how to broach it. *How do you ask a child's mother why the child doesn't know who her father is?*

No, Paul thought, rubbing a hand across his forehead. This wasn't going to be the high point of his day. But it was important, and he prided himself on never putting off things that were important.

There was a painful story behind Angel's plight, he knew

that much. Salford was a small town and almost everyone knew each other, particularly within the church. He'd heard of Marta Rodriguez already. He knew that she was young, having had Angel when she was barely out of her teens, and that she was well respected within the community for the tireless work she did at the local women's refuge. Angel was clearly a well brought up little girl, too. This wasn't a case of neglect. If Marta Rodriguez wasn't telling Angel about her father there was a good reason, which meant this conversation wasn't going to be easy.

Paul tried to think about how it must be for a little girl to not know her father and felt a stab of grief. His own parents had been wonderful but had been killed in a plane crash when he was just thirteen and his little sister, eleven. His parents had been missionaries in Papua New Guinea, which meant that his childhood had been filled with travel and new experiences.

Returning to live in Australia with his aunt and uncle after his parents' death had been another experience, but he'd done his best to get on with his life, look after his little sister and make his parents proud. He often wondered if it hadn't been his early experiences of grief that had pulled him towards chaplaincy, guiding others through their own trials and tribulations relating to the harsher side of life.

A soft knock sounded on the door, pulling him out of his memories. "Come in," he called.

The door creaked open and a young woman with long dark hair entered warily. She looked so much like her daughter that there was no mistaking that this was Marta.

Paul stood to greet her, reaching over his desk to take her hand. It was cool to touch with a surprisingly firm grip for so slight a woman. "Miss Rodriguez, it's good to meet you. Thanks for coming in." He waved for her to take a seat as he sat back down behind his desk.

She perched on the edge of the chair, looking as if she might spring up to leave at any minute while fixing him with intense blue eyes. He noticed the silver cross around her neck.

"Is something wrong with Angel?" she asked bluntly.

Paul took a deep breath and sent up a silent prayer for wisdom. "No, not at all. Angel's a delightful child and doing very well in her lessons."

Marta straightened and pride flared in her eyes.

"However," he continued in a soft voice, "she's been having a few difficulties with some of the other children. They've been asking questions about her father." He waited, praying she wouldn't react adversely to his statement.

She flinched and her eyes seemed to cloud. When she spoke, her voice was clipped. "What questions?"

Paul cleared his throat and shifted in his seat. He smiled kindly, but she didn't return the smile. Instead, she gazed coolly at him. There was a quiet intensity about her that was both intriguing and unsettling.

"It started with curiosity. *What does your dad do?* That kind of thing. But then it became apparent that Angel had no information about her father, and of course the children asked about that. Her teacher and I have told the other children not to tease her about it, but at their age they do question everything, as I'm sure you know."

Marta didn't respond. She wasn't making this easy.

"The thing is," he said, leaning forward and doing his best to sound sympathetic. He *was* sympathetic, but Marta's quiet and almost steely demeanour was unnerving. "Recently Angel has taken to...making things up. Telling the other kids fantastic stories, like her father is a superhero or astronaut. We're worried this will lead to her being teased more. So I thought it might be good for us to have a chat about how we can make it easier for her. I know it must be a really difficult subject."

Marta let out a long, soft sigh and stared down at her empty hands. She was quiet for a long moment, and then she gave a nod to herself as if deciding something. She turned those big blue eyes back to him. "I'm sure you've guessed that she's never met her father. It's not that I've had some wild past and don't know who he is. I don't *want* her to know who he is. She's better off without him in her life."

Paul nodded. He'd thought as much. "I'm not here to judge you, Miss Rodriguez. We just want the best for Angel, and I'm sure you have very good reasons for keeping her away from him, but perhaps she's starting to get to an age where she needs to know why that is." He held his breath, wondering how that had gone down.

Marta shifted in her chair and Paul guessed he'd struck a nerve. He'd be very surprised if Angel hadn't already been asking questions at home.

"It's not an easy thing to talk to her about," she finally said in a monotone voice. "Her father...he was my first boyfriend, if you could call him that. I was naive and he took advantage of that. He was violent." She stopped speaking abruptly and he saw her swallow.

Compassion flooded through him for this woman and her daughter and also anger at the man in question. How any so-called man could treat a woman with violence made no sense to him whatsoever. "I think you're incredibly brave," he said honestly, "and I completely understand why you've kept her away from him. It sounds like the best—and safest—thing to do. But I wonder if it isn't time to have a little chat with her? Explain a little about your reasoning for not saying anything to her until now?"

Marta shook her head sharply. "How do you explain that to a six-year-old?" There was a note of bitterness in her voice.

Paul sighed and tapped his fingers on the desk before replying. He had no children of his own, and he wondered how he would explain it if he were in her shoes. It was one thing to make the recommendation, another altogether to act on it. He shrugged and raked a hand across his dark hair. "I honestly don't know. This must be incredibly difficult for you both, but I do believe she needs to know as much as is appropriate for her age. As I said, the children have questioned her to the point that she's started making things up, which means she's starting to feel ashamed." He spoke as gently as he could. "Keeping her in the dark as she gets older could have repercussions for her emotionally." *And for you too*, he thought but didn't say.

For a second he could have sworn he saw tears in her eyes, but then she blinked and they were gone, so he wasn't sure if it had only been a trick of the light. Even so, his heart went out to her.

"You're right," she said dully. "I always knew I'd have to say something to her one day, but I suppose I wanted to put it off as long as possible. But I know you're right, because I never knew my father either."

Her simple admission, said without emotion, made Paul feel suddenly protective of her. She'd clearly been through a great deal and at such a young age. "The school—and I—are here if you or Angel need any support, with this or anything else," he told her. "And her class teacher will talk to the children again and get any more teasing nipped in the bud."

"But otherwise, she's doing well?" She leaned forward, her eyes a little brighter.

"Yes. The teachers say she's an absolute delight."

Marta smiled for the first time and Paul was amazed at how her features suddenly lit up.

"Thank you," she said, standing to leave. "I'll talk to her after school today."

Paul walked her to the door and shook her hand again. As she turned to leave, he called her back. "Miss Rodriguez? I just wanted to say that I've heard about all the work you do at the shelter. It's impressive. Angel has a great mother."

Marta's cheeks coloured. "Thank you. I don't want anyone else to go through what I did," she said quietly, and then turned and rushed off, leaving Paul to stare after her.

As he closed the door and leaned against it, he exhaled a long breath and uttered a quiet prayer. *Lord God, please watch over Marta and her daughter. Shelter them under Your wings and keep them safe. Let them know that even if their earthly fathers have let them down, that You, their Heavenly Father, will never forsake them.*

Then he sat at his desk and tried to concentrate on the rest of the day's tasks, but he couldn't help thinking about Marta and the sadness behind her eyes, and the way those eyes had shone for just a moment when she'd smiled. It was as though the sun had come out in his small office.

CHAPTER 2

As Marta stood at the school gates waiting for Angel to come out, she thought about the conversation she'd had with the chaplain that morning. She was dreading having to tell Angel anything about her father, but Mr. Peterson was right. She couldn't continue to keep her daughter in the dark about her father, not now that she knew what was happening at school.

She felt terrible that not only had her silence led to this situation, but also that she hadn't known what was going on. *How could she have not known? Was she a terrible mother?* Thinking about it, Angel had been quieter than usual over the past few days, but Marta had put it down to settling into the new school year. Not this.

She'd never wanted her daughter to know the truth about her father, but the chaplain's words had struck a chord. Growing up, she'd longed to know about her own father, but *her* mother had never told *her* anything. Not an iota. Marta had been given her birth certificate when she was left in foster care but had never looked at it. By that point she'd stopped wanting to know, afraid of what she might find.

Liza Rodriguez, her mother, had been an alcoholic and died when Marta was twelve. She'd been a chaotic and unreliable mother, and her alcoholism had often made her neglectful, but Marta had still loved her and took her death badly. Foster care had been lonely and frightening, so when Marta met Steve when she was seventeen and he in his late twenties, she realised she'd been craving love so much she'd ignored the warning bells in her head and fell head over heels. She moved in with Steve without a second thought. However, it wasn't long before she realised what a terrible mistake she'd made. He was a violent man who plied her with drugs, even against her will.

She didn't want that life. The last thing she wanted was to become her mother. Somehow she escaped and ended up at a homeless shelter run by a kind woman named Daisy. She still thanked God to this day for her and her cousin Amy. If it hadn't been for those two amazing women, Marta had no idea how her life would have turned out.

Because of them, Marta and her baby daughter found a home and an adopted family in Salford, a small country town outside of Melbourne. Under Daisy's influence she also found God and a new freedom and love she'd never experienced before. With God's grace she'd managed to build a life for herself in spite of her poor beginnings, and to give Angel the stability her own mother had never given her.

She'd only wanted to protect Angel from any hurt that the past could bring, but now she realised she couldn't wrap her in cotton wool forever. The thought of her making up stories to explain to the other kids why she didn't have a dad made Marta's heart ache.

Marta had also put off talking to Angel about Steve because she simply didn't like talking about him at all. She'd much prefer to keep her past firmly locked away for good, but now that wouldn't be possible. Besides which, without her past, as difficult and horrible as it had been, she wouldn't now have Angel, and Angel was her whole world.

Even so, she was surprised she'd been able to open up, even if only a little, to the chaplain. He had a natural empathy that made him easy to talk to, even though Marta was usually incredibly guarded, especially around men. Since Steve, she often found being around men, especially men she didn't know, uncomfortable and potentially triggering. The only guys she was comfortable around were Amy's husband Angus and their friend Callum, a youth pastor at their church.

When she told the chaplain that Steve had been her first boyfriend, that had been true. What she hadn't said was that he'd been her *only* boyfriend. She couldn't imagine ever being with anyone again. Although she had to admit that she'd surprised herself by noticing how good-looking—and young— the chaplain was. And that she'd noticed. She firmly pushed the thought away. She wasn't going to go there.

"Mum!"

Marta looked up to see Angel running across the playground towards her, pigtails flying. She crouched down and let Angel barrel straight into her arms, squeezing her tight. "Hey sweetheart." She kissed her daughter on the top of her head before standing and taking her hand. "How was your day?"

"It was okay," Angel said.

Marta frowned as a shadow crossed her daughter's face. She sighed. There could be no more putting this off. "How about we go for an ice-cream before we go home? I want to talk to you about something."

Angel's face initially lit up but then grew wary at the second part of Marta's suggestion. "Am I in trouble?" Her big blue eyes, so like Marta's, grew wide with worry.

"Not at all," Marta assured, rubbing her daughter's shoulders. "Mummy just needs to have a chat with you, and I thought it would be nice if we could get an ice-cream at the same time."

Angel's face tilted up, her eyes hopeful. "Can I get chocolate sprinkles on it?"

Marta chuckled, a smile on her face. "Absolutely."

They strolled to the nearby ice-cream parlour where Marta ordered Angel a single cone with chocolate sprinkles, and they sat outside in the parlour's garden. Surprisingly, only two others were there. Teenagers deeply engrossed in their phones while they licked their double cones.

"I went to see the chaplain today," Marta began, trying to sound casual.

"Mr. Peterson? He's nice, isn't he?"

"Yes, he is nice," Marta said hurriedly, surprised to feel her cheeks warm. "He wanted to talk to me about you. First of all, he said you're doing great in your classes, and that makes me very proud."

Angel stopped licking her ice-cream and looked at her mother with a forthright stare. "But?" she challenged, sounding much older than her six years.

She was her mother's daughter all right, Marta thought wryly. She blew out a breath and then continued. "But he told me some of the kids in your class have been asking questions about you not knowing about your father."

Angel seemed to fold in on herself. Both her shoulders and head dropped, and Marta felt sick to the stomach. She should have addressed this sooner instead of burying her head in the sand.

"I'm the only one without a daddy," Angel mumbled, her gaze on her feet.

Marta thought her heart would break.

"And when they ask me why, I don't know what to say so I make stuff up." She looked up. "Am I in trouble for lying?"

Marta blinked back tears. "No, sweetheart, you're not in trouble. We shouldn't make things up, but I understand why you did. And Mummy is so sorry for not talking to you about this sooner. I was waiting until you were older, but now I know that was wrong of me."

She took a calming breath and glanced around to ensure no one could hear. To be doubly sure, she lowered her voice. "Your father's name is Steve, and we lived in Melbourne together for a while. He was Mummy's boyfriend, but we weren't married."

Angel nodded, brushing her eyes with the back of her hand.

"The reason we don't see him," Marta said slowly, wondering how she could possibly make the truth age-appropriate and deciding then and there that some things Angel definitely didn't need to know until she was much older, "is because he wasn't very nice to Mummy. He was quite a nasty man."

Angel frowned and Marta held her breath. Her little girl was clearly weighing up what she'd told her and was trying to process it as best she could. She finally nodded. "Okay, Mummy. I'm glad we don't see him. But I wish you'd told me before and then I wouldn't have been so upset."

Marta swallowed hard and held back tears of regret. How could she have gotten it so wrong? "I know. I really am sorry, sweetheart. If Mummy promises to tell you things you need to know from now on, will you promise to tell me next time you're having problems at school?"

"I promise," Angel said, throwing her arms around her mother.

Marta hugged her tight as relief coursed through her body. She waited expectantly for Angel to ask more questions, but instead, she went back to her ice-cream and told her about her friend Mary's new dress that she'd worn to school that day. Marta smiled gratefully. No doubt there'd be other conversations as Angel got older, but the resilience of small children meant that, for now at least, she seemed to have accepted in stride what she'd been told.

Walking home from the parlour a short while later, Angel continued to chatter away, but Marta's thoughts had turned to her own father. Talking to the chaplain and then Angel about the past had dug up her own long buried feelings about her family. She knew so little about her own father and had never really considered trying to find him. But thinking about it now, she knew it was fear that had been holding her back. Fear of what she might discover. But what if her father wasn't the horrible man she'd always assumed he was? What if he was out there, somewhere, wondering about her?

In the garage there was a box of her mother's things that included her birth certificate. All that Marta had to show for her childhood was in that box. It didn't amount to much, but now she wondered if the box held some clues to the family she never knew.

Whenever she'd asked about her father, her mother had always clammed up and refused to say anything. Marta had resented her for that, but now, after experiencing how hard it had been to talk to Angel about Steve, she empathised. Perhaps her father had been abusive, just like Steve. She shuddered at the thought and wondered if she wasn't better off not knowing, but now that she'd opened that can of worms, she knew it wouldn't go away. She knew her father's name from the birth certificate—David Harris—but that was all. Her mother hadn't even given Marta his name.

When they reached home, a small townhouse within walking distance of the centre of town, Marta left Angel happily playing with her doll's house in her bedroom while she retrieved her mother's box from the garage. A tingle of apprehension ran through her as she sat on her bed and opened it.

Her birth certificate, creased with age and folds, rested on top. She opened it and read the familiar names—Liza Rodriguez and David Harris. There was an address for her father as well. Unit 6/455 Landsborough Parade, Fitzroy, Victoria. He'd been a labourer at the time of her birth. That was all she knew. Feeling a burning curiosity she'd so far repressed, Marta went to her computer and switched it on. Once the internet had loaded, she typed the address into the search engine. Although the chances that he'd be in the same place twenty-four years later were incredibly slim, she felt a flutter in her stomach at the thought of finding him.

When her search revealed that the apartment block her father had lived in had long since been demolished to make way for a modern office complex, she felt a mixture of disappointment and relief. Returning to the box, she lifted out the old photographs from underneath a pile of bills all with different addresses. She and her mother had moved around a lot when Marta was young, Liza never seeming able to settle in one place for long.

She found the picture of her mother and father she'd seen before. She'd looked at it a few times over the years, but never in great detail. Now, with her curiosity piqued, she studied it. Her mother looked young and pretty, different to the way Marta remembered her, which was thin and gaunt from alcohol abuse. Her father had his arm around her and was looking straight at the camera. He was tall and thin with dark hair, and although Marta knew she looked more like her mother, she could see a family resemblance she hadn't noticed before. She traced her fingers over his face, wondering about him and what he was like. There was nothing in the photo to tell her. Other than his height, he was fairly nondescript. She had no memories of him whatsoever and didn't know if she'd ever met him, even as a baby. Or if he even knew about her. Though she guessed he must have been around to be listed on the birth certificate.

The phone rang, cutting through her thoughts. Her friend Heidi's name flashed on the screen. She picked it up and answered it, and when Heidi's warm voice came down the line, Marta found she was glad of the interruption.

"Hey girlfriend," Heidi greeted chirpily. "What are you up to tonight?"

Marta laughed. "The same thing I'm up to most Fridays... watching Disney films with Angel. Why do you ask?"

"Dwayne's having a barbecue since the weather's so nice. Last minute thing. Can you come?" Dwayne was Heidi's boyfriend from church.

"I'd love to," Marta said honestly. After the events of the day, she'd be glad of the company. "It's a bit short notice, though, but I guess I could ask Amy to mind Angel." Her friend Amy always jumped at the chance to babysit. Amy and Angus's five-year-old son, Archie and Angel were as close as brother and sister and loved playing together.

"Do it! You have to come, Marta. Dwayne has a new housemate, and he's super cute."

"Heidi!" Marta laughed again. "You know I'm not interested. Please don't try to matchmake or I won't come." Although she was laughing and knew Heidi meant well, she didn't want to go if she was going to feel like she had to talk to a man she didn't know.

Heidi picked up on her mood. "Sorry. I won't matchmake, I promise. But I do really want you to come."

"I'll try," Marta reassured her. She said goodbye and phoned Amy, telling her that she'd completely understand if it was too short notice, but as she suspected, Amy was delighted at the opportunity to mind Angel.

When Marta told her daughter she was having a sleepover at Amy's, her excitement helped ease the pang of guilt Marta felt. She rarely went out without Angel, even though Amy and her friend Fleur repeatedly told her she needed time to herself sometimes, but she remembered all too well the numerous times Liza had left her to fend for herself. But this was different. Her mother hadn't had good friends like she did.

Amy and Angus, and to a lesser extent, their friends Fleur and Callum, were like family to Marta and Angel. But was it enough? Angel not only didn't know her father, but she had no grandparents or other blood relations either. Although the thought of going anywhere near Steve was abhorrent, perhaps she at least owed it to Angel to try and track down her own father. It was possible she could have siblings out there somewhere, and that would mean aunties and uncles, and even cousins for Angel...

Marta sighed. She was allowing her thoughts too much freedom. She should know not to get her hopes up about such things. She touched the cross around her neck and prayed quickly for peace and guidance. God was her true Father, and it was her faith that had saved her back when she'd been a frightened and vulnerable teenager at Daisy's shelter. God had brought Amy and Angus into her and Angel's life. They'd been so good to them both, and in many ways, they were all the family she and Angel needed.

But she still couldn't stop wondering about her father.

She dropped Angel off and had a quick glass of fresh juice with Amy before she headed to Dwayne's. She didn't know him that well, but he seemed nice and he adored Heidi. Marta was happy for her friend, but at the same time she felt a pang of envy. The only relationship she'd ever had was with Steve and that had left her too terrified to ever try again. Plus, she had Angel to think about. Remembering the string of unsuitable men that Liza had brought in and out of her life, Marta had resolved to never make those same mistakes. If her mother had taught her anything, it was how she *didn't* want to live her life. Yet now Marta wondered if she hadn't allowed that steely determination too much rein, shielding her heart from the good things in life.

She reached Dwayne's front door and tried to shake off all thoughts of her father and mother. It would be nice to simply relax and have a good time without all those worries. For once she'd try to simply be in the moment and have fun. Heidi was good for her. A naturally bubbly, friendly girl, she hadn't let Marta's usual reticence put her off, and before she'd known it, Marta found that Heidi had become her best friend. Something else she'd never had before moving to Salford.

As she waited at the door, she checked her reflection in the glass. She'd put on a new white blouse, dark blue jeans and strappy sandals—a big change from her usual sneakers. Her dark hair curled softly around her shoulders and she'd even added a little lip gloss and mascara. She couldn't help noticing that she looked nice, even though it felt prideful to admit it.

She smiled as the door opened, ready to greet Heidi or Dwayne.

Except it wasn't either of them who stood there.

It was Mr. Peterson, the chaplain from Angel's school.

CHAPTER 3

Marta stepped back in surprise. Was she at the wrong house?

"Miss Rodriguez?" The chaplain frowned, though there was a twinkle in his eyes.

Dressed in a simple polo shirt and cargo pants, he looked relaxed and handsome. She took in his closely cropped dark hair, friendly amber eyes, full lips and hint of a dimple. A little too clean-cut for her, maybe, but still... She felt herself blush and said quickly, "Err, I'm sorry. I was looking for Dwayne."

The chaplain's frown deepened, and then he grinned. "Oh, you must be Heidi's friend."

"You know Heidi?"

"She's my housemate's girlfriend."

Of course. This was Dwayne's new housemate. Marta shook her head, marvelling at the coincidence as the chaplain stepped aside to let her in, calling for Heidi as he did so.

"It's Paul by the way," he told her.

Marta smiled shyly. "And I'm Marta."

Heidi barrelled into the hall in a cloud of perfume and hugged her. "You made it! I'm so glad. This is Paul, Dwayne's housemate."

"We've met," Marta said. "He's the chaplain at Angel's school."

Heidi rolled her eyes. "Duh. I should have realised you would know each other. I didn't think. Well, that saves me doing the introductions. Come and get a drink." She looped an arm through Marta's and led her through the kitchen and outside. Paul followed along behind. Marta felt self-conscious and almost painfully aware of his presence.

Outside, Heidi went to help Dwayne with the barbecue, leaving Marta standing awkwardly next to Paul. When they both started to talk at the same time, they stopped and laughed, which seemed to ease some of the tension that had been building.

Marta chuckled. "You first."

"I was going to ask after Angel. I hope I didn't upset you earlier… It's obviously a really difficult subject and I wasn't sure how to tackle it, particularly with being new to the school."

"I thought you handled it very sensitively," Marta said honestly. "And you were right. I had a chat with Angel on the way home."

"Oh? How did that go?"

Marta felt flattered by the genuine interest Paul showed. It was only because he was Angel's school chaplain, she knew, but even so, it was nice that he was so obviously concerned about their welfare.

"It was...okay, I think. I didn't tell her too much. Just her father's name and that it's been best not to see him since he wasn't very nice." Marta hesitated, not wanting to reveal too much. She didn't want Paul to pity her. She hated being pitied. "I was really worried about her reaction, but she seemed to take it in her stride. Giving her a few simple details seemed to placate her...for now at least. But now that I've opened that channel of communication, she knows she can come to me with any further questions."

Paul looked at her with soft eyes that made her lower her gaze. "You're very brave," he said softly.

Marta felt a warm fizzing in her stomach. She liked him, she realised with a start.

"You look deep in thought," Paul said.

Marta blinked and tucked a piece of hair behind her ear before lifting her gaze. She hoped he couldn't tell what she'd been thinking. "Yes." She laughed lightly. "I was thinking what a coincidence it is, you living here with Dwayne. Will you be coming to our church, then?" The thought of seeing him on a regular basis, as part of her community rather than just through Angel's school, made her feel both apprehensive and strangely excited.

"Most likely. I haven't been the last few weeks as I've been moving things from Melbourne. I might be there Sunday, though. It depends on if I drive back to visit my aunt and uncle tomorrow. My aunt's making noises about a farewell lunch even though I officially moved weeks ago."

"That sounds lovely," Marta said.

Paul was about to say something else when Heidi returned, chattering excitedly, then dragged Marta off to meet more people. She glanced back at Paul over her shoulder. He was still watching her. She smiled shyly and shrugged before disappearing with Heidi into the crowd of young people from their church.

The evening passed quickly. Although she had a great time, she didn't get the chance to speak to Paul on his own again, because he excused himself and went inside early, stating he needed an early night if he was going to drive to his aunt and uncle's place in Melbourne the following morning.

Marta tried to swallow her disappointment. She wasn't really interested, she told herself. She wasn't interested in men at all. Nevertheless, thoughts of Paul and his kind smile kept her awake most of the night.

CHAPTER 4

Sitting in church two days later, Marta was finding it hard to concentrate. Usually she listened attentively to the sermon and always found it had relevance for her life, but today she couldn't stop thinking about the possibility of finding her father. Once she'd made her mind up about something she did it with her whole heart, and at some point between taking out Liza's box and this morning, she had indeed made up her mind.

She'd prayed early that morning, asking God for guidance to help her find her family, and for the strength to cope with whatever she discovered. After some time in prayer she'd felt more at peace, but she was also more certain that this was something she had to do.

So far, though, her searching had been less than fruitful. She'd looked through the white pages and found that there were over a thousand D. Harris's listed in Melbourne. Facebook had been the same, and even after trawling through hundreds of profile pictures, the photo that she had was too old and blurry to be much help. People could change a lot in twenty-four years.

But she wouldn't give up. Later, once Angel was in bed, she would start phoning the list of numbers she'd gotten from the white pages. It would take a lot of time, but she would do it.

With a start, she realised the sermon was coming to an end. She stood and sang the final hymn along with the rest of the congregation, and then went to fetch Angel from Sunday School, feeling guilty for not paying attention. She also tried not to dwell on the fact that Paul hadn't been there. He must have decided to visit his relatives after all. It sounded as though he was very close to his family. Marta couldn't help feeling a twinge of envy.

As she was coming out of Sunday School with Angel, Amy waved them over. Marta walked towards her friend and they hugged. As usual, Amy smelled of floral perfumes and cookies and Marta guessed she'd been baking. Her stomach rumbled. She'd felt too antsy that morning to eat breakfast, so Amy's next words were more than welcome.

"Would you like to come over for lunch?"

"We'd love to. I really need a chat, too," Marta confided.

Amy raised a brow and nodded. "Of course. Angus can mind the kids for a while."

Marta smiled gratefully. She could always rely on Amy and felt blessed to have such a good friend.

They sat on Amy's back deck a short while later, laughing at Angel and Archie spraying Angus with water guns in the backyard.

Amy leaned back in her chair and looked over the top of

her glass. "So, what do you want to talk about? I can tell from your face that you aren't simply wanting a new cookie recipe."

Marta gave a wry smile. "You know me too well. But yes, you're right." She blew out a slow breath and twiddled with a lock of hair before she answered quietly, "Angel's started asking questions about Steve."

Amy's eyes widened. More than anyone else, she would understand why that would be such a sensitive subject. It had been Amy and Angus who'd found her the last time Steve attacked her, jeopardising Angel's life while she was still in Marta's womb. "Well, I suppose it was always going to happen. What did you say to her?"

Marta told her about the meeting with Paul and her subsequent conversation with Angel.

Amy nodded thoughtfully. "It seems you've handled it really well. I know how hard this must have been for you, dragging up all those old memories. But Angel will have to know the truth someday."

Marta nodded. "I know. I suppose I wanted to put it off for as long as possible. But then after Paul...Mr Peterson...told me she'd been getting upset at school, I couldn't stop thinking about how *my* mother always refused to tell me anything about *my* father and how hard that was. So," Marta took a deep breath before continuing, "I've decided to try and look for him. To find him."

Amy blinked. "Your own father, you mean?"

When Marta nodded yes, Amy wrinkled her brow, looking deep in thought.

"What is it?" Marta asked, sensing her friend was reluctant to say what was on her mind. "Do you think it's a bad idea? I've been praying about it, and I feel like it's something I need to do."

"Then you should definitely do it," Amy assured her. "Just please promise me you'll be careful. I don't want to see you get hurt. The thing is...if you think about the reasons you didn't want to tell Angel about Steve..." Her voice trailed off, but Marta knew what she was thinking. What if the reason Liza hadn't told Marta about David was the same as Marta's reasons for keeping quiet about Steve? What if he too, had been abusive and dangerous?

"I know," Marta said quietly. "I know that's a possibility. In fact, thinking about the kind of men my mother used to bring home when I was a child, it's more than a possibility, it's a probability. But it's time I knew. There's always been this huge question mark in my life, but I've always ignored it. I suppose because I was scared of what I might find. But now I need to find out what I can. It might not be that bad... I might even have family out there somewhere." Marta winced as she heard the longing in her own voice.

"I understand," Amy said. "Just be careful, okay? And I'm here for you, whatever happens."

Marta leaned forward and embraced her friend, feeling grateful for Amy's simple kindness. Regardless of what she might discover, Amy and Angus would always be family to her and Angel. They'd been through too much together for it to be any other way.

LATER, after Marta read Angel a bedtime story, prayed with her, sang to her and said goodnight to all her teddy bears before the little girl finally fell asleep, Marta picked up the list of all the D. Harris's she'd printed out that morning. By the length of it, she guessed it would take a few hours to even make a dent. Still, she had to start somewhere.

Three hours later, she went to bed exhausted. Not one of the names she'd phoned had claimed to have ever lived at the address she'd given, or to have known a Liza Rodriguez. For all she knew she could find her father and he could lie anyway, not wanting the past dragged up. After all, if he were alive, he could also have a new family and not want anything to do with her.

She dropped Angel at school the next morning and then drove to work, her thoughts still on the list. She hadn't even got a tenth of the way through the names. There had to be an easier way, but so far she couldn't think of any.

From the outside, Salford Women's Refuge looked like nothing more than a big town house, or rather, two town houses that had been knocked into one. Only an astute eye would notice the discreet security cameras and the extra locks on the doors.

Marta loved her job. Although sometimes she found the stories the women disclosed about their lives triggering, reminding her of her own experiences, it was those very experiences that made her so empathetic and helped the women open up and trust her.

It was also Marta's way of giving back. God had been so very good to her and her life had turned around so spectacularly, so how could she not pass that on to others who were in the same situation she'd once been in? Every time a woman went through the refuge and moved on to a better life, Marta felt a piece of her own heart heal. Of course, every time a woman went back to the perpetrator, which unfortunately happened all too often, she felt a piece of her heart break. She knew all too well what it was like to have the person who hurt you also be the only one you thought could ever love you.

Now, thanks to God, Angel, and her friends, she knew that real love was unconditional and kind, not hurtful and abusive. It was about compassion, not control. Of course, she had no other experiences of romantic love.

As the face of Paul Peterson drifted into her mind, Marta's heart constricted. She really had to stop this. He was the chaplain at Angel's school! Yet she couldn't deny she felt drawn to him. Maybe it was an indication that she was finally facing her fears, but the thought of dating anyone, even someone as nice as Paul, still terrified her.

The businesslike voice of the refuge manager, Vanessa Hargreaves, cut through Marta's thoughts as she hung her jacket up in the utilities room. "Marta. Could you come into my office for a moment?"

"Sure." She frowned, wondering what Vanessa wanted. She followed her into her office and sat on the chair opposite her.

Marta got on well with Vanessa, a trim woman in her forties who ran the refuge with the perfect mix of kindness and order. She was very self-contained and not one to make friends with the staff, but Marta admired her and often got the impression that the feeling was mutual. Certainly, Vanessa always seemed happy with her work.

"I've had a request this morning, Marta, and I've put your name forward," Vanessa told her.

"Request?"

"Yes." Vanessa leaned forward, a smile on her face. She looked almost excited, Marta thought. "The chaplaincy board sent an email. You know we have a few Christian girls' schools in the district. Salford and beyond?"

Marta nodded. Where was this going?

"Well, they've asked if one of our support workers could visit each of the schools and give a talk to the girls about relationships."

Marta frowned until she saw the expectant look on Vanessa's face and realised what she meant. Her eyes widened. "You want me to do it?"

"Of course. Who else would be better?"

"I know nothing about relationships." What was Vanessa thinking?

Vanessa smiled sadly. "But you know the types of men to avoid. And you know about healing, and moving on, and coming to the Lord. Your story is incredibly powerful, Marta. Don't underestimate yourself. I think you could have so much to offer these girls. You're an incredible role model."

"You really think so?"

"I know so."

Marta didn't know how to respond. The thought of getting up on stage and telling her story to a school full of teenage girls was nerve-wracking to say the least. Yet...maybe Vanessa was right. Maybe she could inspire the girls by sharing her testimony. Not only warn them about toxic relationships, but witness to them of God's healing and redemptive power. After all, although the schools themselves were Christian, not all of the pupils knew God's redemptive love.

"Can I think about it?" she asked. This was something she wanted to spend time praying about. Not rush into.

"Of course," Vanessa replied. "I know it's a very personal thing I'm asking you to do. But I believe God uses us to inspire others and turn even our worst experiences to good. Let me know as soon as you can."

Marta promised that she would, then excused herself. She had a busy day ahead, helping a new woman settle in, working on the helpline and then leading a support group in the afternoon. As the day wore on, she was glad it had been full, because it stopped her from thinking about Vanessa's surprise proposition, the list that awaited her at home that evening, and the possibility that one of the names on it might be her father. And Paul.

That night she put off making phone calls as long as she could. She helped Angel with her homework and after putting her daughter to bed, did chores that could have waited. If she left it any later she wouldn't be able to phone at all, so she finally picked up her list and began.

The first number she called rang with no answer. The second was a Deirdre Harris. The third call, however, was different.

A man answered the phone.

"Hello," Marta began. "I'm looking for a David Harris."

"Yeah. Speaking," said a gruff voice.

Trying to stay calm—'David' was no more unusual a name than 'Harris', Marta thought, although her heart was beating in her throat. "I don't suppose you used to live at Landsborough Parade? And know a Liza Rodriguez?"

There was a brief silence, then, "Yeah. That's me. Who's asking?"

Marta's hands trembled. She was talking to her father! She tried to answer but her mouth had gone so dry that she couldn't speak and her stomach began churning.

"Hello?" he said again. Before she understood what she was about to do, she panicked and disconnected the call. She stared at her phone, willing herself to call him back, but she couldn't bring herself to do it. She wasn't ready. Instead, she quickly prepared for bed and crawled under the covers with her heart still hammering in her chest.

She couldn't sleep. She tried to read but the words swam on the page. Although reciting her favourite psalm and praying calmed her a little, sleep continued to elude her. In the end she got up and padded quietly into Angel's room, slipped under the covers next to her daughter's warm body and snuggled up with her.

Angel murmured in her sleep then relaxed into Marta's arms. Marta put her face in her daughter's hair and breathed in her scent and immediately felt soothed. Angel's presence was like a balm to her agitated soul.

As she finally began drifting off, she resolved to phone the man back the next day and have the conversation she needed to have. She also had an hour in the morning between the school run and starting work. She'd use that time to go swimming. That always helped clear her head.

With a plan in place she felt better and finally fell asleep after wondering what the next day would bring.

CHAPTER 5

Paul cut through the water, his shoulders burning after a few laps of doing the butterfly stroke. He would switch to front crawl soon, but he liked to challenge himself. His father had always said, *keep your body strong and your mind will follow suit,* and after all these years, Paul still followed that particular piece of advice.

He sorely missed his parents, but he also felt grateful for the wonderful childhood they'd given him and Melody. Although the grief of losing them had been intense at such a young age, he also felt it had helped shape him into the man he was today. It had certainly influenced his decision to become a chaplain. Originally studying teaching at university, the call to ministry had nagged at him until he decided to do a chaplaincy post-graduate course. He'd always had a strong faith, instilled in him initially by his parents and then his aunt and uncle, and he knew it had helped him stay strong through the turmoil of the loss. God was truly the great Healer.

He saw so many people buffeted by the storms of life: sickness, death, grief and trauma, never realising that God could be their anchor if only they would let Him. Paul had known it was his calling to help guide people through those storms and had done his final year's placement at a hospice before getting the job at Salford Christian School. He was surprised by how much he enjoyed working with the children, and at twenty-six, he felt very fortunate to have figured out the trajectory of his life path early on.

Only the relationship area of his life was lacking, he thought ruefully. He'd had one long term relationship throughout university with his first and only girlfriend, but they'd split when it became clear she wasn't keen on the idea of him going to Bible College. She'd been pulling away from her faith as Paul's had been growing, and although sad, he'd felt relief when they parted amicably. If he were honest, his heart hadn't been in the relationship for some time. Although he hadn't become bitter over his parents' death, he did often wonder if he'd locked a little of his heart away, shielding it from further loss. He hadn't had a relationship since, or even felt anything more than friendship for a woman.

Until Marta Rodriguez.

He hadn't stopped thinking about her all weekend, and as much as he tried to tell himself that it was only concern and sympathy that drew him to her, he knew it was more than that. Something about her intrigued him. She seemed quiet and completely unaware of her beauty, yet he detected an almost steely strength in her, too. Just like him, he suspected there were parts of herself that Marta locked away, probably even more so. From the little she'd told him and her obvious devotion to her work at the refuge, she'd clearly been through some horrific experiences, yet her devotion to her daughter was plain to see. Paul admired her deeply and hoped he'd see her again at church, or at Dwayne's, where he could simply be himself rather than the school chaplain.

As he swam, he prayed for her and Angel, the rhythmic motion of his strokes and the lapping of the water helping him feel at ease.

Heavenly Father, wrap Your arms around Marta and Angel. Help them to know that they're loved, truly, by You. Give Marta strength and courage, and spread your wings over little Angel and keep her heart safe.

Reaching the end of the pool and knowing he needed to change strokes before his shoulders gave out, Paul stood for a quick breather and lifted his goggles. Slipping into the lane next to him was a young woman with dark hair twisted on top of her head. "Marta?" he asked, his jaw dropping.

She looked around, startled, saw him and burst out laughing. She looked pleased to see him, he thought. "Paul? What on earth are you doing here?"

When he raised a brow and looked down at himself, she laughed again. "Okay, swimming, obviously."

He shook his head, hardly able to believe they'd bumped into each other again. Another piece of advice his father always used to give him...*in God's world, there are no coincidences.* "I often swim in the mornings before work. It helps clear my head. Sometimes I even find it's a great opportunity to pray."

Marta nodded enthusiastically. "Me too! I usually come on a Monday since I don't start work until later in the morning. It gives me a rare bit of time to myself."

He smiled sympathetically, thinking how hard it must be for her, bringing Angel up alone. Still, she was clearly doing a great job. "If you've got time," he said before realising what he was about to say, "perhaps we could grab a quick coffee before we go to work."

Marta blinked, then hesitantly said yes. "I'll get a few laps in first, if that's okay," she said, and then took off in her lane. Her strokes were smooth and her long arms cut the water cleanly as she powered down the pool. She was a pleasure to watch.

Thirty minutes later they sat in the Leisure Centre café drinking coffee together. Paul couldn't help thinking how pretty Marta looked after her swim, with her cheeks flushed from the exertion and her dark hair escaping in damp, curly tendrils from its bun. He looked away quickly as her gaze met his, not wanting her to think he was being too forward. He'd already surprised himself by asking her for coffee, but then he'd thought, what were the odds that they kept chancing upon each other? Salford wasn't that small. He couldn't help wondering if God had put her in his path.

But if He had, Paul was sure it was so he could help her, not fall for her. "Do you have a lot going on at work today?" he asked. "I imagine it must be a very demanding job."

"Probably no less demanding than dealing with the spiritual needs of an entire school." She smiled, but then said more seriously, "But yes, some days can be very difficult." Then her face lit up. "Oh, did you know I've been asked to speak to the high school girls?"

Paul smiled. He'd known that the refuge had been approached for a speaker, but not that Marta's name had been put forward. But now that he knew, it made perfect sense. He had no doubt that she'd be fantastic at it and he told her so.

"Thank you. I do want to do it, but it feels like a huge responsibility and, well, I don't talk about my experiences very often. I don't like to." A shadow crossed her face and Paul felt a pang of empathy and the sudden urge to protect her.

"Perhaps it will be good for you too," he suggested gently. "Pray on it?"

"Yes," Marta agreed. "I will. I meant to spend some time reflecting on it last night but...well, I've had something else on my mind."

Paul waited, wondering if she'd tell him what she meant but not wanting to pry.

Marta absentmindedly curled an escaped wet tendril of hair around her finger, staring into the distance before she said in a rush, "Talking to Angel about her father really made me think. I know so little about my own family, and of course, they're Angel's family too, aren't they? So I've decided to try and find him."

Paul blinked, thinking back over what she'd just said. "Your father, you mean?"

She nodded. She was chewing her lip anxiously and Paul realised the subject had turned her into a bag of nerves.

"I spoke to someone last night who said he was David Harris—that's his name—and that he used to live at the right address and knew my mother. It must be him. Except..."

"Except?" Paul prompted as she looked down as if suddenly embarrassed.

"I disconnected the call. I freaked out, thinking that it was really my father on the other end of the phone. I've probably blown my chance now. He didn't ring back."

"You could ring him again."

"Yes. That's what I decided to do. I'm going to try again tonight. I suppose I'm just nervous about what I might find."

"I understand. It's a huge thing to do. Seek God's guidance, Marta. He'll have a plan for you in all this, even if it doesn't quite seem clear yet."

"Thank you," she said softly, taking a sip of her coffee.

"Where does he live?" Paul asked. "In Salford?"

Marta shook her head. "No, Melbourne. That's where I was born."

He had an idea. Before he could change his mind or talk himself out of it, he said, "That's where my aunt and uncle live. It looks like I'll be going down again this weekend because my uncle's throwing my aunt a surprise fiftieth birthday party. If you contact this guy by then, maybe you could come along for the drive. There's plenty of room at my aunt's—she's very much a 'more the merrier' type of person. I'm only thinking it might be safer than going on your own, if that's what you were planning," he added. "After all, you don't know anything about this guy."

"Or if he's even telling the truth," she added.

"That too. I don't see why he would lie, but I suppose you never know."

"That's really kind," she said, although her gaze didn't quite meet his. "I'll definitely think about it, and I'll see what David says, if I can get him to speak to me again. I could ask Amy to mind Angel...although I would feel bad. She had her on Friday so I could go to the barbecue."

"How often do you do that? I'm betting once in a blue moon."

"Yes," Marta nodded. "You're right. Well, I'll give it some thought."

There was an awkward silence before Paul looked at the clock and realised he was about to be late for work. The time had flown by. "I'd better go," he said reluctantly. He really didn't want to leave her.

She got up and walked out with him, exclaiming that she too hadn't realised the time.

Paul walked her to her car. "Let me know what happens, and have a good day at work."

"I will. You too." She drove off with a wave.

Paul stood and watched until her car disappeared around the corner. He thought about her quest to find her father and hoped for her sake it would be successful. He really did want to help her.

Praying for discernment and wisdom, he got into his own car and drove to school, ready to start another day.

One that he already knew would be consumed with thoughts of a certain dark-haired young woman.

CHAPTER 6

"Marta, have you made a decision yet?" Vanessa asked as she poked her head into Marta's office.

She looked up from the case file she was studying and frowned. All day at work she'd been wildly distracted, debating whether or not to call back the man she suspected was her father, and also by thoughts of Paul at the pool this morning. "Sorry? A decision?"

Vanessa let out a heavy sigh. "Yes. About speaking at the schools?"

Marta felt guilty as she realised she'd barely thought about the offer again since mentioning it to Paul that morning. "Sorry, Vanessa, I haven't decided. Can I have a little more time?"

Vanessa barely suppressed a tut. "I know it might seem daunting, but I do need to know by the end of the day or I'll have to ask someone else." Her face softened as she smiled. "I really would like it to be you, though. I feel you have so much to offer these girls."

"Thank you. I'll let you know before I go home today. I promise." She glanced at the clock as Vanessa left the office. That didn't give her long to think about it at all. She had a one-on-one with a new resident, Penny, who had arrived that morning, and then would barely have time to type up her notes before picking up Angel from school. Quickly, she prayed for guidance. *Lord, help me to make the right decision, motivated neither by fear nor pride, but only by Your will. In Jesus' precious name. Amen.*

She then walked to Penny's room and knocked on the door softly. Penny was only nineteen, and when Marta greeted her that morning, she couldn't help but be reminded of herself when she left Steve all those years ago. The girl had seemed quiet and frail, but she also had a harder, more defensive edge to her that Marta recognised too. Vanessa had assigned Marta as Penny's keyworker, perhaps noticing the similarities herself.

Penny opened the door and looked blankly at Marta. There were faint shadows of bruises around both her eyes and Marta felt her stomach twist. "Hi Penny. We're scheduled for your first one-on-one?"

"Will it take long?" the girl asked abruptly, her eyes unsmiling. She had long dark hair and was desperately thin. Marta tried not to take the rudeness personally. She understood the girl's instinct to push anyone away who tried to help.

"No. One-on-ones are usually weekly for an hour, but the first one is simply for me to get to know you a little better, and there's a form I need to go through. So maybe twenty minutes?"

Penny sighed audibly. "Fine," she said, and opened the door for Marta to come in.

Marta stepped inside the small room and felt a pang of sadness. Penny's rucksack lay on the bed. It was all the girl had brought with her. She'd fled in the early hours of the morning while her abusive partner was snoring off his latest drunken binge and had grabbed what she could. National Women's Aid had brought her here to Salford just before the start of Marta's shift. Penny looked exhausted and Marta guessed she hadn't slept much, if at all.

Penny sat on the bed while Marta sat at the small table by the window. The room was pleasant enough, but basic. Salford Refuge relied largely on charity funding and donations, so while it was clean and smart and certainly cared for, it was hardly the lap of luxury. Their residents came from all walks of life, from homeless young people like Marta had been to affluent women whose husbands hid their violence behind a respectable facade. Working here, Marta had quickly learned that money was no indicator of happiness.

She went through the form methodically, noting down Penny's circumstances and her specific needs. Penny answered her questions in a monotone voice, giving away no more information than she had to. Marta's heart went out to her, and on a sudden whim, she pushed the form away. "Penny," she said softly. "It's going to be okay."

Penny stared at her, wide-eyed, then her eyes suddenly filled with tears. "How do you know?" Her voice had lost its bitter edge and she now just sounded desperately sad.

How much should she tell her? She'd always been careful to maintain professional boundaries, knowing she couldn't get emotionally involved no matter how much she wanted to befriend some of the women who came through the refuge. Yet she also knew that there were times when a touch of personal disclosure could help forge a connection with a resident who was otherwise reluctant to engage. No matter how well trained or qualified the support staff, sometimes what someone like Penny really needed was for someone to say to her, "Me too."

"I was in a similar situation years ago," Marta said, weighing her words carefully.

Penny's forehead creased. "Really? You? You seem so…normal."

Marta laughed. "Thanks…I think. But yes, I entered a halfway house for women when I was seventeen and fleeing a violent man. So I do have some understanding of how scared and angry and confused you must be feeling right now. But I promise you, it does get easier. You can heal and go on to have the life you deserve, even if that seems a million miles away right now."

Penny wiped her eyes. Since Marta had spoken, her whole demeanour had changed and softened. "Thank you," she said sincerely. "It does help to know I'm not the only one. And to know that there's hope."

Marta got her papers together briskly before she started crying herself. "Any time you need to talk, give me a shout. You don't have to wait for our session—we're quite flexible here."

Penny thanked her again and Marta left, thanking God as she walked down the stairs that He had enabled her to not only come through her own dire situation, but put her in a position to help other women.

As she finished her prayer, she knew that she had to say yes to Vanessa.

Vanessa looked delighted when she told her just before she left work for the school run.

"If you need any tips, make sure you ask," her boss told her, "but honestly, I know you'll be amazing. Have faith in yourself. Or better still, have faith in the Lord. He brought you here for a reason, Marta. I thoroughly believe that."

"Thank you." It was all she could say.

As she drove to the school to collect Angel, she felt butterflies in her stomach, although she wasn't sure if they were more from excitement or anxiety. There was no doubt she felt incredibly honoured and proud to have been asked, but her fears of getting it wrong or her talk not being good enough nagged at her. And she had no idea what to say...*I'll just have to pray on it*, she told herself firmly. She believed what Vanessa had said—that God had led her to this. Talking to Penny had convinced her that this was exactly what she was meant to be doing. She only wished that the thought of speaking about her experiences on stage wasn't so anxiety-provoking.

Angel ran into her arms and her spirits lifted. She'd noticed that since their talk about Steve the other day Angel had seemed in lighter spirits. While she knew there would be more difficult conversations in the future and Angel may not always accept things so easily when she got old enough to truly understand, things were better for now, and she was grateful for that at least.

They spent a relaxed evening doing Angel's homework—a dinosaur poster—and then watching cartoons after homemade pizza, which Angel chose the toppings for. Then Marta tucked her in bed, said her goodnight prayers with her, and went downstairs.

And stared at the phone.

If she was going to call the man back who claimed to be David Harris, she needed to do it before her fears got the better of her. She had to know. She remembered Paul's offer for the coming weekend and decided to take the bull by the horns. She'd already made one tough decision today, she thought determinedly, so she may as well carry on while she was on a roll.

Taking a deep breath, she picked up the phone and dialled the number.

The same voice answered. "Hello?"

"Mr. Harris? It's Marta Rodriguez. I phoned you last night and you said you knew my mother."

There was silence for a few moments before the man said tentatively, "Yes, that's right. I knew Liza. Very well, in fact. We were together for a while."

It's him. Her heart beat wildly in her chest.

"Who are you?" he asked, and Marta thought he sounded suspicious, which she supposed was to be expected.

"I'm Liza's daughter. And...I...I believe I might be *your* daughter. At least, a David Harris with your old address is listed on my birth certificate."

There was a long pause during which Marta could hear the man breathing heavily. Then he abruptly said, "Where's Liza now? Is she there?"

"She passed away," Marta said quietly. "Twelve years ago."

There was another silence. Marta didn't know what to say.

What did one say in a situation like this? Was he upset about her mother's death?

When he next spoke, however, he sounded quite upbeat. "Well, we should meet then, shouldn't we? Get to know each other. Where do you live?"

Marta thought about telling him Salford, but hesitated. Even if he was her father, she knew nothing about him, or why her mother had left him and then never told her anything about him. "I can come to Melbourne on Saturday, if you're free. We could meet in a café."

"Okay," he said eagerly. Maybe he was just excited about the prospect of meeting his daughter, Marta thought, but she couldn't shake the fact that her instincts were warning her to be careful.

They arranged to meet at a café in the Bourke Street Mall on Saturday at noon. The mall was a busy, public place, so if she felt at all uncomfortable or intimidated it would be easy enough to leave. Even so, she still felt wary, and as they said goodbye to each other and ended the call, Marta wished she'd asked him more questions. What if he was lying and he wasn't really David Harris? Although she couldn't think of a reason why that would make any sense. She wished she'd asked more questions about Liza's life to confirm she really had the right person, but then she realised with a pang of grief that she didn't know enough about her mother's past to even do that.

She couldn't go on her own if she felt this unsure. She could almost hear Amy's voice telling her not to be so foolish. To keep herself safe. So, she phoned Paul.

He sounded delighted to hear from her and her stomach did a little flip. On the phone his voice sounded low and deep and made her heart skitter. "How are you?" he asked. "Is everything okay?"

"Yes, but I wanted to ask you about your offer this morning." She told him about her conversation with David and how she believed he was her father based on the information she had, but she had misgivings about meeting him. "So I wondered if it would still be alright to hitch a ride with you on Saturday and back on Sunday? I can get a hotel Saturday night. There are lots of cheap ones in the area. I would stay with Amy's cousin Daisy, but I remember Amy saying she's away this week."

"Of course it's fine. It'll be great to have your company on the drive."

At the thought of being on her own in the car with Paul for a few hours, warmth flowed through her. She also realised that she instinctively trusted him, for it wasn't like her to volunteer to spend time with men she didn't know well or feel comfortable with. Perhaps that was the source of her discomfort around meeting her potential father. She didn't know him at all.

"But I won't hear of you staying in a hotel," Paul continued. "I mean, it's up to you, but you might not want to be on your own after such an emotional day. Come and stay at my aunt and uncle's. They'd love to meet you. My sister Melody is staying in the double room. You can bunk with her."

That did sound nice, Marta thought. She couldn't help feeling curious about Paul's family and wanting to find out more about him, so, she agreed. As she ended the call, her head was whirling. It had been quite a day.

CHAPTER 7

The week passed in a blur as Marta tried to focus on Angel and work, but the coming weekend loomed over her. She also received her speaking schedule and panicked a little when she saw that it would begin the following week, and her first school would be Salford Christian Secondary—where Angel would one day go. She tried to sit down in the evenings and plan her talk, but she couldn't stop thinking about Saturday and the fact that she might finally get to meet her father. Emotions warred within her.

What if, as she suspected, he was a man like Steve? Or what if he'd been married when she'd been conceived? She had so many questions and there were so many possible outcomes that her head spun every time she thought about it. She prayed every evening but couldn't shake the gnawing feeling that she may have set something in motion that she would later regret. But she had to know.

Saturday morning came and Marta dropped Angel off at

Amy's and waited for Paul. When he beeped the horn, a wave of panic raced through her. This was really happening. She gave Angel a big squeeze, feeling a pang of separation anxiety at the thought of leaving her daughter for the night while she was in Melbourne. While Angel had stayed at Amy's a few times before, she was usually only a few blocks away, not a three-hour drive. Angel hugged her back and then skipped off happily to play.

When Marta straightened, Amy was smiling at her. "She'll be fine...don't worry."

"I know," Marta said and hugged her friend again. "I'm just really nervous. What if I go all that way and he doesn't show?"

"It's in God's hands," Amy said firmly. "Just promise me you'll stay in a public place...just in case."

Marta promised, swallowing her sense of foreboding, and then hurried outside. She slid onto the passenger seat next to Paul. He looked fresh and handsome in a smart lemon polo and dark chinos, and for a moment she wished she'd put something smarter on than her long skirt and tie-dyed vest.

"You look lovely," he said, and then he coughed awkwardly as though he hadn't meant to say it. "I mean, very summery. It's a lovely day, isn't it?"

"It is," she agreed, smiling to herself at his sudden shyness. *He likes me too*, she thought, as her stomach began fluttering. As if she wasn't nervous enough already.

Yet she felt safe with Paul, she reflected as he drove off. She would never have agreed to three hours in the car with him otherwise. There was something about him that put her immediately at ease. At the same time, her growing attraction to him made her feel acutely self-conscious around him.

They made small talk for a while, then he put the radio on and they travelled in comfortable silence before stopping at a rest station for water and to stretch their legs. As she got back into the car, Marta saw the sign for Melbourne. In under two hours they'd be there. She might finally get to meet her father. She sucked in a breath to steady her nerves, trying to hold on to Amy's words and simply trust God that whatever the outcome, it would be okay. She also tried to ignore the growing sense that maybe she was doing this more on her own volition than God's. She'd made the decision to find her father, and she had a steely determination when she wanted something. A childhood of living on her wits had made sure of that.

"How are you feeling about the meeting?" Paul asked as they continued driving.

Marta sighed. "Honestly? Really anxious," she confessed. "What if I've got this all wrong and it isn't even him? The more I think about it the more something doesn't feel right. But if I don't go and meet him now, I'll never know and then I'll always be kicking myself with regret."

Paul nodded thoughtfully. Marta realised that in the times he'd mentioned visiting his aunt and uncle, he hadn't once mentioned his own parents.

"Will your Mum and Dad be there this weekend?" she asked tentatively, hoping she hadn't put her foot in it, even though she couldn't imagine Paul having any kind of dysfunctional family.

He didn't answer immediately, but when he did, his voice was quiet. "My parents died in a plane crash when I was thirteen."

Marta gasped. "I'm so sorry, Paul," she said sincerely.

"Thank you. It was hard, as I'm sure you know. But I was lucky in that my aunt and uncle took both me and my sister Melody in, and they're wonderful people. So I try not to feel sorry for myself. As much as I miss my parents, I had a great childhood."

Marta couldn't help feeling a pang of envy even in the midst of her empathy for his grief. After her mother died, she had been shuffled around the foster care system until she met Steve when she was sixteen. She shuddered, and Paul seemed to notice it.

"I'm sorry," he said, glancing at her. "I hope I haven't brought up any bad memories for you."

"You haven't. This whole situation has though, I suppose. I think that's probably why I've never really thought about looking for my father before. I didn't relish the idea of dragging the past up. But after I spoke to Angel about my ex, it kept nagging at me. So perhaps it's time to confront the truth. Whatever that turns out to be."

Paul was quiet for a moment, then said, "I think you're incredibly brave."

"Brave?" Marta felt her cheeks colour at the praise.

"Yes, absolutely. To have come through everything that you have and be such a good mother and do the work that you do..."

"It's God. Not me."

Paul smiled. "I don't doubt it. But you clearly have a great deal of God-given courage and resilience, too. Do you never give yourself credit for anything?"

Marta felt herself blush even more. She seemed to have permanent red cheeks around this man. "I guess I'm still working on my confidence," she said. Then, wanting to change the subject as well as curious to know more about him, she asked him more about his own background. "So, your parents and their family are from Melbourne?"

"Yes, but I actually grew up in Papua New Guinea. My parents were missionaries."

"Wow! That must have been pretty incredible."

Paul chuckled. "Yeah, it had its moments." He regaled her with tales of his childhood in PNG and Marta listened with rapt attention. Paul wasn't just a nice man. He was funny and interesting too, and she really enjoyed his company. For a while, she even forgot about the impending meeting with David Harris.

"It sounds lovely," she said, "and your whole family seems really close. I want that for Angel. I suppose that's another reason I'm trying to track my father down, because she has no blood relatives in her life except me. Still," she said as Paul shot her a look of sympathy, "I'm incredibly blessed to have Amy and Fleur and their families. They feel like blood even though they're not. Especially Amy"

"It's love that creates the strongest bonds," Paul said, "not just genetics. They *are* your family, and you're also part of God's family. That's the greatest bond of all."

"Yes," Marta agreed. "Ever since I let the Lord into my life, I've really learned what love is. Faith turned my life around."

Paul turned and smiled at her. For a moment their gazes locked and a look of deep intimacy, almost vulnerability, passed between them before he hastily turned his gaze back to the road. *What was that?* Marta felt slightly dazed. Even if it was only to be one of strong friendship, she couldn't deny that there was a natural connection between Paul and herself.

THEY ARRIVED in Melbourne nearly half an hour before she was due to meet David. At least by being early she'd have time to make herself comfortable in the café and get a coffee, she thought, rubbing her hands on her skirt as she felt her palms going clammy.

"Are you ready?" Paul asked, turning to meet her gaze. "It's not too late to change your mind about this if you're having any doubts."

"No," Marta said stubbornly. "I'm ready."

"Okay." Paul nodded and glanced at the clock on the dash. "I'm going to make myself scarce and take a run along the Yarra River. It's not far, so as soon as you call me, I'll come and get you. If you need me at any point, just call."

"I'll be fine," Marta replied lightly. She was used to looking after herself, but there was no denying she was pleased by Paul's obvious desire to protect her. She took a deep breath and smiled before she got out of the car.

Holding her head high, she walked through the mall until she located the café. Being a Saturday, it was busy enough that she wouldn't be alone with this man who, relative or not, was a stranger to her, but not so busy they wouldn't be able to talk privately.

She ordered a coffee and sat down, tapping her nails on the table as she watched the clock. Would he recognise her straight away? She assumed he would…she looked like her mother, after all.

Just before noon, a dark-haired man walked into the café and looked around. Marta straightened, her heart hammering, but then decided it wasn't him. He wasn't tall enough to be the man in the picture, plus, he was overweight.

But then he spotted her and narrowed his eyes. "Marta?"

She nodded.

There was a look of excitement in his eyes as he rushed over.

It must be him. Perhaps he looked taller in the picture because he was standing next to her mother, who had been quite petite. Yet something about him immediately made Marta feel uncomfortable.

He slid onto the seat next to her. "It's so good to see you," he said. He had piggy little eyes that bored into her.

She tried to smile back.

"You look just like her," he said as he looked her up and down in a way that made her feel defensive. She tried to tell herself to give him a chance and her reaction was just nerves, but something in her felt repulsed by him.

"How was your journey?" he asked.

"It was great. I came with a friend," she said quickly, not wanting him to think she was alone.

Disappointment momentarily flashed across his face before he shifted closer. "I was thinking we could go back to my place and get to know each other."

Alarm bells went off inside her head. There was no denying it, the way he was staring at her wasn't the way a father would look at his daughter. This man couldn't be her father, surely?

She scanned his face. Although the photo was old and

blurry, there wasn't any resemblance other than the hair colour. Neither did she see anything of herself in him.

Noticing her studying him, he winked.

Marta recoiled. "You're not my father," she said flatly, the disappointment a crushing weight in her stomach.

Seemingly unconcerned at being caught, the man shrugged. "Maybe not. But let's not waste the afternoon, eh? You look like a girl who likes to enjoy herself." He started to trace his finger down her arm before she jerked her arm away.

Marta's nostrils flared. "Is your name even David Harris?"

The man shrugged. "I've just moved in. The old tenant was called that, I think, but he was too young for what you're looking for, love. A father figure, that's what you want."

Was he mentally ill, or just a chancer? She stared at him. "Why would you pretend to be someone you're not?" She felt genuinely bewildered. And sick.

Then, to her horror, he placed a sweaty hand on her leg. "Love, I can be anyone you want me to be," he said as he squeezed her thigh.

Marta panicked. She jumped up and threw her still hot coffee into his lap.

He yelped as the hot liquid hit his jeans. He grabbed Marta's wrist, hard, his eyes glittering with malice.

She wrenched her wrist from his hand, grabbed her bag and fled. She ran out of the café, out of the mall and down three streets, sobbing the whole way. Only when she was satisfied he wasn't following her did she stop and sink down into an alcove next to a newsagent. She took her phone out of her bag and with her hands shaking, phoned Paul.

He picked up on the first ring.

"Paul, come and get me…" Her voice broke on a sob.

"Marta? Where are you, what's happened?" Paul sounded panicked.

She looked around for a street sign, told him where she was and hung up. She crouched in the alcove, shaking, until she saw his car.

He pulled up, leaned over and opened the door for her. His eyes were wide with concern. "What happened?"

She stammered out the whole story.

His face grew dark, and he looked around as if trying to locate the man. When Marta dissolved into tears again, he pulled her into his arms and let her cry, stroking her hair and making soothing noises.

She cried into his chest, grief and fear and embarrassment welling inside and flowing out. It wasn't like her to cry like this in front of anyone, even Amy, but she was so shocked by what had just happened and so relieved to see Paul that she couldn't hold back. Eventually her sobs subsided and she pulled away, but she couldn't meet his gaze.

He passed her a tissue he pulled from the glove box.

"I'm sorry," she said, blowing her nose.

"You haven't done anything wrong."

"I feel so stupid." Why hadn't she listened to her instincts? Deep down, especially in her prayer time, she'd known this wasn't right, but her determination to learn something about her family, about Angel's family, had overridden her common sense.

"You're not stupid. That…man…" Paul spat the word through gritted teeth. "He obviously saw an opportunity to take advantage of a young woman. The fault lies squarely with him. Do you want to go to the police?"

Marta shook her head. "They can't arrest him for being a sleaze...or for lying. Unfortunately. Can we just get out of here?"

"Yes. It's about half an hour's drive to my aunt and uncle's. Let's get a drive-through coffee on the way, shall we? Settle your nerves a bit."

Marta nodded and settled back into her seat as Paul drove off. She felt weary and hollowed out with shock, but she also felt extremely thankful that Paul was with her.

Thank You, Father, she prayed silently, *for bringing this man into my life. I don't know what I would have done without him today. Forgive me for not heeding Your voice...I was stubborn and wanted to do things my way. I'm so sorry.*

As she prayed and Paul continued to drive, peace settled over her. She was silent for the rest of the journey, closing her eyes and resting in the reprieve. She reflected again on how safe she felt with Paul, even after such a nasty shock. It was a strange feeling for her, safety not being something she'd had much of in her life.

She opened an eye and studied his profile as he drove, glancing away when he swung his gaze towards her. The day had been a disaster so far, but at least she would get to spend more time with this man who was quickly capturing her heart. That thought filled her with warm fuzzies and helped her forget her disappointment.

CHAPTER 8

Marta smoothed down her skirt and sat gingerly in the pew between Paul and his sister Melody. Paul's family's church was more traditional than her church at Salford and she felt out of place in her hippy-ish clothes, even though Paul had assured her she looked great and the whole family had made her feel welcome.

In fact, staying the night with them had been bittersweet, reminding her of what she'd missed out on in her own life and making the disappointment at not finding her father even sharper. However, it had been impossible to feel downcast for long as everyone had been so friendly. When they arrived, Marta almost changed her mind about staying. Their house was so large and modern. Paul's family was more affluent than she'd expected. Yet, she'd been welcomed with such warmth, which was surprising considering she was a last-minute guest and they didn't know her from a bar of soap, and she soon felt at ease.

She'd shared a room with Melody, who'd told her stories about their childhood in PNG, and how hard it had been after she and Paul lost their parents. When Melody described how brave he'd been and how he'd been entirely focused on supporting her, pride for him welled within Marta. She knew he was a good man, but now she was learning just how good he was.

As she was settling down to sleep, Melody asked, "So, how long have you and Paul been dating? I'm so glad he's finally met someone."

Marta's mouth had dropped open and she sprang up. "Dating? We're not dating. Paul is...a friend. He's the chaplain at my daughter's school. I had something I needed to do in Melbourne this weekend so he suggested I come along. I didn't realise you thought..."

Melody laughed. "Really? That's what Paul told us too, but we thought he was just being tight-lipped. Especially when you both arrived."

Marta frowned, Melody's comments confusing her. "What do you mean?"

Melody lowered her gaze and shrugged, as if embarrassed. "Well, the way you both look at each other... It seems you like each other." She angled her head. "Don't you?"

Marta hadn't known what to say. Yes, she did like him and knew she had to start being honest with herself about that, but could Paul really feel the same way? Seeing how nice his family and home were only made her feel inferior. What did she, a single mother from the wrong side of the tracks, have to offer a man like him? And yet, deep down she knew Melody was right. Paul didn't look at her as though she was inferior at all. In fact, he seemed to have nothing but admiration for her.

Marta had gone to sleep with her head whirling with the events of the day. Now, thinking about last night's conversation with Melody, she was acutely aware of Paul's presence next to her in the pew, his thigh nearly touching her own. She'd been quiet over breakfast and knew Paul thought she was still upset about yesterday, but mostly she'd felt embarrassed at the thought that his family all assumed she was his girlfriend.

As though she didn't have enough to worry about. She was due to give her first talk at the school the following day and hadn't prepared at all. She would have to do some work on it when she got home and after putting Angel to bed. Marta was looking forward to cuddling her daughter, having never been away from her for so long.

The service began with a few hymns, some Marta knew and some she didn't, and then the notices. When the pastor stood and began reading the Bible passage, the sinful woman in Luke, one of her favourite stories, a tingle flowed through her and she felt with all her heart that she'd been meant to be there that morning.

When one of the Pharisees invited Jesus to have dinner with him, the pastor began reading, *He went to the Pharisee's house and reclined at the table. A woman in that town who lived a sinful life learned that Jesus was eating at the Pharisee's house, so she came there with an alabaster jar of perfume. As she stood behind Him at His feet weeping, she began to wet His feet with her tears. Then she wiped them with her hair, kissed them and poured perfume on them.*

When the Pharisee who had invited Him saw this, he said to himself, "If this man were a prophet, He would know who is touching Him and what kind of woman she is—that she is a sinner."

Jesus answered him, "Simon, I have something to tell you."

"Tell me, teacher," he said.

"Two people owed money to a certain moneylender. One owed him five hundred denarii and the other fifty. Neither of them had the money to pay him back, so he forgave the debts of both. Now which of them will love him more?"

Simon replied, "I suppose the one who had the bigger debt forgiven."

"You have judged correctly," Jesus said.

Then He turned toward the woman and said to Simon, "Do you see this woman? I came into your house. You did not give me any water for my feet, but she wet my feet with her tears and wiped them with her hair. You did not give me a kiss, but this woman, from the time I entered, has not stopped kissing my feet. You did not put oil on my head, but she has poured perfume on my feet. Therefore, I tell you, her many sins have been forgiven—as her great love has shown. But whoever has been forgiven little loves little."

Then Jesus said to her, "Your sins are forgiven."

The other guests began to say among themselves, "Who is this who even forgives sins?"

Jesus said to the woman, "Your faith has saved you. Go in peace."

Marta smiled as the reading came to an end, allowing the words, and God's message of unconditional love and forgiveness, to wash over her. She listened keenly as the pastor gave a sermon that could have been fashioned just for her.

"Many of us can be like the Pharisee, judging those we think are 'more sinful' than us, and so cut ourselves off from God's love. That's why Jesus told us to pray, *Forgive us our sins so that we may forgive those that sin against us.* But often the truth is that deep down most of us feel more like the woman with the jar than the Pharisee.

"We all have our secret sins, our shames, our situations or wounds that make us feel we're not good enough. That we're not worthy. But in this story, the Lord tells us that this is not true. We're all worthy of being loved by the One who has the power to forgive all sins, wash away all hurts, heal all wounds.

"All we need to do is as this woman did—throw ourselves at His feet and pour out all that we have without letting our pride or our unworthiness hold us back. For this is how God invites us to come to Him...fully, without holding anything back, just as we are. No matter how broken the world has made us feel, no matter how 'bad' we think we've been. Jesus paid for *all* our debts when He died on the cross, and what He asks of us is our love. For it's not our righteousness that saves us, but our faith."

As she felt the Spirit's presence, Marta closed her eyes and for a beautiful moment felt how truly loved she was by God, and how her thoughts of inferiority were not true, not in God's eyes, anyway, and they were the only eyes that mattered. A wave of gratitude welled within her.

She suddenly knew exactly what she needed to say to the girls the following day.

After the service they had a quick lunch at Paul's uncle and aunt's before setting off for home. Before Marta got into the car, Melody gave her a big hug and winked at her. Marta's cheeks felt flushed as she slipped in onto the passenger seat.

"What was that about?" Paul asked.

Marta hesitated but decided to be honest. She was sure Melody would question him about her at some point if she hadn't already. "Melody thought we were dating. I tried to tell her we're not, but I'm not entirely sure she believed me."

Paul coughed into his hand as he pulled away from the kerb. "My aunt and uncle assumed the same. But you should be flattered. When I told them you weren't my girlfriend they were *most* disappointed." He glanced at her and gave a shy smile. "They both thought you were lovely."

Marta swallowed hard. "Thank you," she murmured, not knowing what else to say. There was an awkward silence until Paul broke it by turning the radio on. She laid her head back against the seat and closed her eyes, enjoying the feeling of the sun shining through the window and onto her face.

"You seem a lot more at peace today," Paul commented after a while. "I was worried yesterday after that horrible incident with that man."

Marta opened her eyes and nodded. "It *was* horrible, but I've had such a good time since that I haven't had much time to think about it. I really enjoyed church this morning, and the sermon was beautiful. It gave me a lot of inspiration for the talk tomorrow."

"I forgot it was tomorrow! Are you nervous?"

"Yes! But a lot less now than I was. I think I was truly meant to hear that message this morning."

Paul smiled. "God always finds a way to tell us what we need to hear."

She groaned. "If only I'd listened before agreeing to meet that man. I had a bad feeling on the phone, but I pushed on, regardless."

Paul glanced at her with sympathy. "You tried. If you hadn't, you'd never have known if he was your father. And I don't think you should give up your search if finding your family is important to you." He cleared his throat and Marta thought he seemed nervous. "I don't want to intrude, but Marta, if you'd like my help, I'm only too happy to support you in this. If you need a lift again or just someone to talk to...I'm here."

"Thank you," she said quietly, overwhelmed by his obvious concern. "I have no idea where to start again, though. I could trawl through that huge list of D. Harris's I suppose, but how do I prevent the same thing from happening again?" Quite apart from the potential danger, Marta wasn't sure she could cope with a string of disappointments like yesterday.

"What about your mother's family?" Paul suggested. "They must know something about your father. Do you have any information on them?"

Marta shook her head sadly. "No, and I've never met them. All I know, since my mother alluded to this a few times when she was drunk, is that they disowned her when she took up with my father. Which I suppose should tell me all I need to know about him."

"Not necessarily. And people can change. But it might be something to consider—tracking your mother's parents down. Do you have your mother's birth certificate? That would give you some information about them, and where they were living when your mother was born."

"I haven't got it. But I could order one from the Department of Births, Deaths and Marriages." Hope sprung in her again and she beamed at Paul as a surge of affection flowed through her. He looked over and grinned back and for a moment, their gazes met before he turned back to face the road. A warm tingle flowed around her heart. Perhaps Melody hadn't been far off the mark at all.

It seemed Paul's family weren't the only ones to assume there was something between them. When they arrived at Amy's place, Amy invited them in for a slice of cake. Marta needed to get home to finalise her speech for the next day, but she also knew how good Amy was at baking, so they both accepted the invitation.

After they'd finished their cake and Marta had filled both Amy and Angus in about her trip, Paul sat chatting with Angus in the lounge while Marta helped Amy take the used plates to the kitchen. Angel and Archie were playing happily on the deck.

"Sooo..." Amy said as she loaded the dishwasher. "How are things going with Mr. Handsome?"

"Amy!" Marta hissed, checking behind her to ensure the men hadn't heard. She shut the kitchen door before turning back to Amy. "We're just friends, honestly. But he's a really, really nice guy."

"And a handsome one."

Marta chuckled. Amy was irrepressible. "Yes, okay, and a very handsome one."

"Glad to see your eyes are still working. So, you're friends, but you like each other, right? It sure seems that way."

"Paul's family thought the same thing. But he hasn't said anything. I don't know, Amy, I think he's just being nice. He *is* a chaplain. It's kind of his job to be nice."

"His job does *not* involve taking you to meet his family, or helping you find yours, or looking at you like he's never seen a woman before," Amy retorted.

"Do you really think he looks at me like that?" Marta couldn't deny how pleased she felt at the thought.

Amy nodded. "Yes. And Marta, if I can be honest with you a moment..."

"Of course." She wondered what her friend was going to say.

"You can't be on your own forever. Steve was a long time ago, and you deserve to meet someone who really cares about you and Angel. Maybe it's time you took a chance?"

Marta inhaled sharply. But she knew Amy was right. And she *did* like Paul. Yet the thought of getting into a relationship still filled her with fear.

"Pour it all out to God," Amy suggested, echoing the sermon from that morning.

"That's not the first time I've heard that today," Marta said quietly.

"See!" Amy grinned, her eyes sparkling with amusement. "I'm right."

Marta thought about Amy's words as Paul drove off a little later and wondered what it might be like to date him for real.

"He's very nice, isn't he Mummy? Is he going to be your boyfriend?" Angel asked cheerily as she skipped down Amy's driveway towards the car holding Marta's hand.

Marta couldn't help but laugh. *Okay God, I get it.*

Later on, after Angel went to bed, she would spend some time in prayer. Not only about her talk the next day, but about Paul and the possibilities for the future that were taking shape in front of her.

CHAPTER 9

Marta woke in a lather of sweat, panic welling inside as the shadows in the room loomed large around her.

Another bad dream... She squeezed her eyes shut and breathed deeply before glancing at the digital clock. Three in the morning. She sighed. All night her sleep had been fitful and broken. She felt ill—shaky even, with a creeping sense of nausea that made her wonder if she'd eaten something funny.

Perhaps she would have to call in sick and miss the talk. The minute she had the idea, she felt the temptation of it and immediately felt a little better. Why subject herself to such a nerve-wracking experience when she was feeling poorly and should probably stay in bed?

Yet something didn't sit right with her. Yesterday she'd been so certain about what she needed to say and that God was guiding her in this, and she'd felt sure she was meant to give the talk to the girls at Salford High. Had she been wrong? It wouldn't be the first thing she'd gotten wrong recently, she thought, remembering Saturday's disastrous meeting with the man claiming to be David Harris. Perhaps God was telling her not to do it after all, and she was simply being prideful to think her story was worth telling and could make a difference. After all, her past was hardly something to be proud of.

She sat up and rubbed her temples. As the fog of sleep cleared from her mind, she knew something wasn't right. Bad dreams and feelings of worthlessness were definitely not messages from God, but perhaps something more sinister. She recalled a sermon she'd heard recently on the concept of spiritual warfare. Perhaps that's what was going on inside her. Turning on her lamp, she reached for her Bible, trying to remember the passage the pastor had read about protecting against spiritual attacks. Something about spiritual armour...Yes, that was it. Ephesians 6...

Finding the right passage, she read it slowly, her voice quiet but clear in the still room. As she read, her head cleared and the words sank into her like a healing balm, imbuing her with strength and courage.

Be strong in the Lord and in His mighty power. Put on the full armour of God, so that you can take your stand against the devil's schemes. For our struggle is not against flesh and blood, but against the rulers, against the authorities, against the powers of this dark world and against the spiritual forces of evil in the heavenly realms.

Therefore put on the full armour of God, so that when the day of evil comes, you may be able to stand your ground, and after you have done everything, to stand. Stand firm then, with the belt of truth buckled around your waist, with the breastplate of righteousness in place, and with your feet fitted with the readiness that comes from the gospel of peace. *In addition to all this, take up the shield of faith, with which you can extinguish all the flaming arrows of the evil one. Take the helmet of salvation and the sword of the Spirit, which is the word of God. And pray in the Spirit on all occasions with all kinds of prayers and requests. With this in mind, be alert and always keep on praying for all the Lord's people.*

Marta sat silently for a moment then closed her Bible, bowed her head and prayed.

"Lord, thank You for giving us Your Word that we may use it as a shield and sword in times of trouble. Thank You for Your eternal love and the refuge it provides. Help me to find the right words tomorrow, for if even one pupil hears something that is of benefit, I will have done Your work. Keep me strong against the self-doubt and lack of courage, and instead help me to remember that I am Your beloved daughter and against Your power no evil can stand."

As she turned off the lamp and lay back down, she realised the shakiness and nausea had gone, and she was confident they wouldn't return, at least not to that degree. She went to sleep and slept soundly until her alarm woke her to get Angel up and dressed for school.

The day of the talk had arrived.

While Angel ate breakfast, Marta prayed and read through the passage again. She felt so much lighter as she dropped Angel to school and made her way to the high school. As she was buzzed through reception and taken down to the auditorium, the butterflies in her stomach were very active. She reached up and touched the cross around her neck and silently prayed for calm.

The principal, a kindly looking woman with short grey

hair, greeted her warmly. The auditorium was large and had been partitioned off. A group of around fifty schoolgirls sat in front of a small stage.

Her eyes enlarged as she recognised the man standing on the stage. Paul! How had she not realised he'd be there? Now she was really nervous. But this wasn't about Paul. It wasn't about her, either. It was about these girls and how her journey might help them on theirs.

He grinned at her as she walked onto the stage and stood next to him, her hands trembling. The sullen looks some of the girls gave her did nothing to encourage her confidence.

As the school's chaplain, Paul gave a short introduction which Marta barely heard, her heart was pounding so loudly. Then, before she knew it or was ready, he turned to her and held out the mike.

Taking it, she thanked him and then turned to face the girls seated in front of her. They were aged from fifteen to eighteen, and most looked either bored or were openly sneering at her. Marta's heart began to pound. At that moment, she wished she was anywhere but there. She offered a silent prayer that she would find the words these girls needed to hear. The prayer grounded her.

She breathed deeply and began, her voice hesitant at first. "Good morning. I'm Marta Rodriguez, and I've been invited here to share my story with you."

The girls continued to look bored and one girl directly in front of her actually rolled her eyes.

Marta sighed. She had to be direct with them, she knew. She recognised her teenage self in their sullen faces. "I was a drug addict," she said bluntly. That got their attention—even the eye-rolling girl looked shocked and sat straighter, looking at Marta intently now.

"My mother was an alcoholic. I never knew my father. Mum died when I was twelve, although, to be honest, I was used to looking after myself by then anyway. I thought I was on my own in a world that didn't want or understand me, and so I toughened up as best I could. I became the 'bad girl'. The rebel. I guess I thought if I pushed people away—good people, anyway—then they couldn't let me down or hurt me."

All the girls were attentive now, and her misgivings fell away as she got into her stride and shared the rawest parts of her past with these girls who were on the cusp of womanhood and all the risks that came with it. Especially for those who were most vulnerable.

"I was shunted from foster home to foster home," she continued. "So I closed myself off to avoid rejection. Of course, that meant that when I was placed with a nice family who really tried to care for me and offer me guidance, I did everything I could to sabotage it. I was the girl I thought no one wanted and I told myself—lied to myself—that that was just fine with me.

"Of course, it was a lie. Deep down, I craved love. It was all I really wanted. And so, I was easy pickings when an older guy came into my life when I was only sixteen." She paused. Her heart had started to hammer at the thought of sharing the story of her time with Steve. *Give me courage, Lord,* she prayed. She sensed Paul's gaze on her and knew he was also praying. That knowledge gave her comfort and courage.

"At first I thought he loved me," she said softly, "but he put me through hell. He was violent and abusive. He plied me with drugs to control me. Then I discovered I was pregnant."

A hush had settled over the auditorium. The girl in front had tears in her eyes.

"One day I managed to escape and I ended up in a homeless shelter. The woman who ran the place not only cared for me, but she spoke about unconditional love, about a Father who had always watched over me, and something inside me started to heal.

"But," she took a deep breath, "I still had a lot of unresolved issues. I hadn't fully surrendered to God in my heart and I still craved Steve as much as I was terrified of him. I'd come to love my unborn baby and all I could think of was how much I wanted a family...and so I went back to him, believing his promises that he'd change. Instead, he beat me up as punishment for leaving. I was so desperate to escape the pain and humiliation I overdosed on drugs. My baby and I almost died."

A cold shiver spread through her as she remembered that time. She paused to gather her swirling emotions before she continued. "But we didn't die. The wonderful friends I'd made through the shelter searched for me and found me, and I gave birth to a beautiful baby daughter. I went to rehab for a while, and then, when I was released, I learned to be a proper mother to her. She's such a precious gift from God." Marta couldn't help but smile, and she realised that most of the girls were smiling too.

"I reconnected with God, properly this time, finally allowing His love to fully penetrate my heart, right down to the depths where all the bad stuff from my past lingered, eating away at me. God used Angel, my daughter, to open my heart to love, and I knew then that I wanted to help others who found themselves in similar situations to those I'd been in, so as soon as Angel was old enough, I went to college.

"Now I'm a support worker for women fleeing abusive relationships, and I know I'm exactly where God wants me to be. Sometimes I look back at the girl I was and I know that if I had my time again, I'd listen to the few people who did try to guide me—teachers and my foster family—instead of being so consumed with anger and fear. But I'll never regret having my daughter, and I know that everything that has happened to me only made me stronger. God never left me. He had a plan for me all along. Just like I know He has a plan for each and every one of you girls, even if it doesn't feel like that right now.

"Sometimes I fall into the trap of feeling ashamed of my teenage self. But then I remember how fiercely loved I am. And so, if there's one thing I want to say to you today, it's this: don't let anyone make you question your self-worth. You are God's beloveds, precious in His sight. It doesn't matter what you look like, what your background is, what you've done or what has happened to you. You are loved. And I encourage you to love yourselves and treat yourselves with respect."

Tears sprang to her eyes as applause filled the auditorium. "Thank you. I'll be here for a while if anyone would like to talk —strictly in confidence, of course. Or you can write down your details and pass them on and I'll arrange a support session."

She handed the mike back to Paul. Undisguised admiration and pride filled his eyes. "That was amazing," he whispered, then he turned to face the girls and invited them to join him in prayer. He prayed for Marta, offering gratitude for her amazing story before praying a blessing over all the girls that they too might come to know God's transformative love in a personal and real way.

He then dismissed the girls. Although none came forward there and then, many scribbled their names and numbers on the sheet she'd left on the table by the door, including the girl who had tears in her eyes. Marta felt humbled as she understood that she had indeed made an impact.

The principal was ushering the girls out, leaving her and Paul on the stage alone. At the naked admiration still shining in his eyes, Marta felt suddenly awkward and gathered her things together. "Er...I'd better go. It's going to be a busy afternoon at work. Thank you for your support today."

"I thought your talk was incredible," he said sincerely. "It resonated with me too."

"Really?" Marta's brows drew together, his words surprising her. After all, their backgrounds could hardly be more different.

"Yes." He nodded. "Obviously, I haven't overcome the things you have, and I'm not nearly so brave, but I do know what it's like to feel alone as a youngster and see the world as a dark place. After my parents died...well, I've never really spoken about it to anyone before, but I really struggled, emotionally, and with my faith."

Something in her softened as she looked at him. She remembered Melody telling her how strong he'd been, but he must have been grieving silently. He'd been strong for his sister, which was most admirable, but in doing so, had ignored his own grief. "I guess we all have our dark nights of the soul," she said quietly.

Their gazes locked for a moment, and then Paul smiled, breaking the tension. "I wondered," he paused and rubbed the back of his neck, "if you'd like to do some laps together at the pool this week?"

She nodded eagerly. "That would be lovely. Angel has her swimming lessons tomorrow afternoon after school, if that works for you?"

"Perfect." He smiled.

Marta headed back to work with a song in her heart. Not only had her talk with the girls gone well, but now she had a sort-of date with Paul. It was only swimming, but she was beginning to think both Melody and Amy were right. The chemistry between them couldn't be denied any longer.

Although she felt the familiar panic at the thought of dating, she touched her cross and took a few deep breaths as she walked towards the car. *If this is Your will, Lord, and I'm not just getting giddy because he's so nice, then let me not allow fear to prevent me from following the path You've laid out.*

As she pulled away in her car, however, she had a sudden image of Steve, snarling in anger, and felt herself flinch. She recited Ephesians 6 silently and the image receded.

It's okay, she told herself. *You're safe. And Paul is not Steve. You never have to see Steve again.*

Or at least, she hoped she didn't.

CHAPTER 10

Perched on the side of the pool waiting for Marta, Paul slapped his feet against the edge, a sure sign he was anxious. After listening to her speech yesterday, he couldn't hide his feelings for her any longer, least of all from himself. Marta was simply the bravest, most beautiful woman he'd ever met, and he also saw the more tender side of her that she tried so hard to hide.

He'd spent a long time in prayer the previous evening asking God to reveal His heart and to show him if Marta was truly 'the one'. He certainly felt she was, and during the peace that had come over him in prayer, he'd been certain God's answer was 'yes'.

Only afterwards, after becoming absorbed in the hustle and bustle of life, did the doubts start to creep in, although deep down he knew they were more about his own fears rather than anything else. The same fears that had kept him so resolutely single the past few years. He knew all too well the bitter sting of loss, and although he'd never grown bitter or questioned his faith, he realised now he'd allowed himself to develop an avoidance to love. Now that it was staring him in the face, he didn't quite know what to do.

When he was with Marta, it all seemed so simple. It had felt so natural to have her at his family's house on the weekend and he'd loved watching her interact with them and felt a warm rush of pleasure at seeing her getting on so well with Melody. As if she were part of the family. And yesterday, listening to her speech and seeing the way the schoolgirls had hung on her every word, hearing the passion in her voice, he'd had no doubts. If he let her slip through his fingers, he would regret it forever. It had seemed the most natural thing to ask her to meet him for a swim. Now he glanced at the clock and wondered if she was even coming.

"Paul!"

He needn't have worried. He looked up to see her coming into the pool area, a smile on her pretty face, and rose to greet her.

"Sorry I'm a bit late. I was just making sure Angel was settled in her swimming class."

In her simple one-piece swimsuit, with her hair pulled up in a bun and curly dark tendrils falling softly around her face, she looked gorgeous. He averted his gaze from her slim figure as she approached. He wasn't the sort of guy to stare at a woman, even one as beautiful as Marta. Especially Marta. "Don't worry. I've only just arrived myself." He dismissed her apology with a wave of his hand.

They slipped into the pool, each in a different lane and began to swim. As he'd noticed before, she was an excellent swimmer, only just behind him, and he waited at each end for her as they did a few laps. "You're an impressive swimmer," he said.

"Thanks." She grinned. "I've always loved the water."

They got out after forty minutes so she could collect Angel from the indoor pool where the lessons were being held.

"Where are you off to now?" he asked, trying to sound casual as he towel-dried himself.

"Just taking Angel home for dinner."

"Would you like to take her to the burger and ice-cream place down the road? My treat."

Marta hesitated, then smiled warmly. "I'd love to, thank you."

Paul showered and dressed quickly and then waited outside for Marta and Angel. They appeared, flushed and with damp hair, Angel chattering excitedly about her lesson. He smiled at her fondly and was pleased when she grinned back.

"Mummy says you're taking us for burgers and ice-cream," she chirped.

"That's right."

"Can I have one of the double ones with the strawberry sprinkles?"

"Angel!" Marta said, her eyes wide with horror.

Paul laughed. "Why not? I might just join you."

"Bet I can eat more than you."

Paul shook his head. "No way. I am the absolute ice-cream eating *champion*."

Angel giggled and grabbed Marta's hand as they headed towards the burger joint. It was a casual diner in a retro style with an outdoor eating space with a kids' play area. It opened onto a field with a small river running through it. After ordering, they took their seats and Angel ran off to check out the climbing frame.

"You did so well yesterday. Your talk was phenomenal," he said.

"Thank you. I really enjoyed it. Vanessa has scheduled a few more for me this week at other schools and I've got to follow up with the one-on-ones from yesterday."

"It sounds like a lot of work on top of what you already do at the refuge."

Marta shrugged. "It is, I suppose, but I can manage it. I really feel this is a path I'm meant to go down."

"I don't doubt it. You're a wonderful inspiration."

Their gazes met and Marta smiled shyly. She looked young and innocent, her world-weariness momentarily dropped. Warmth flowed through him as he gazed at her. *Ask her out*, a voice in his head whispered. *Ask her out.*

He was about to do so when the burgers arrived, and then Angel ran over for her food. *Later*, he told himself, knowing that if he didn't take the plunge and ask soon, he might never do it at all.

Angel chatted about her day while they ate, then Paul took her inside to choose the biggest ice-creams they could find.

Marta gasped as they came out with them in their hands, shaking her head but laughing. "Angel Rodriguez," she gently reprimanded. "Your teeth will fall out!"

"They won't, Mummy," Angel said seriously. "I'll be careful to clean them."

Marta and Paul met each other's gazes and giggled.

After ice-creams, Angel wanted to see the river, so they

took a slow walk along the riverbank while she skipped happily in front of them. Paul snuck a look at Marta's profile, noting how the evening sun formed a golden haze around her hair and brought out the blue of her eyes. Realising Angel had gone a little way ahead, he turned to Marta, trying to gather his courage to ask her out, but before he could do so, she called Angel back, scolding her for running off. Paul didn't know whether to laugh or groan in frustration as his second attempt was thwarted.

Third time lucky, he told himself as they walked back to their cars. He bid Angel goodbye, watching as Marta strapped her into the back seat of her car. When Marta straightened, he took a deep breath. "Marta?"

She angled her head, her forehead scrunching. "Yes?"

"I was wondering," he began, then fell quiet, his mouth suddenly dry. When she raised a bemused brow at him, the rest of his words tumbled out in a rush… "What you are doing on Friday? There's a new film opening at the cinema, and if you can get someone to watch Angel, I'd love to take you."

Marta's mouth dropped open momentarily and Paul thought she was going to say no. He was steeling himself for the rejection when she finally replied, "Yes. I'd really like that."

Trying and failing to stop a grin from splitting his face ear to ear, he nodded excitedly. "Great! I'll pick you up about seven?"

"Perfect."

There was an awkward silence where they both just stood, staring at each other, before Marta cleared her throat. "Well, I'll see you Friday, then." She climbed into her car.

"Yes. Friday." Paul waved at Angel as Marta pulled away

from the kerb, and the little girl, ice-cream still on her mouth, waved back happily. He watched Marta's car until it reached the bottom of the street, turned the corner and disappeared.

Friday, he thought as he turned and walked back to his own car, floating on cloud nine.

CHAPTER 11

"Marta, take a few days off next week. You've been working too hard," Vanessa said, catching her on the way out at the end of the day. It was Friday, and while she'd been looking forward all week to her date with Paul, she was absolutely exhausted. She'd done two more talks that week, followed up with three one-on-ones, and to top it off, it had been a busy week at the refuge. If she hadn't been so excited about going out with Paul, she might well have cried off and had an early night.

"Thanks. If the roster allows, then I might just do that." Marta smiled gratefully as she left.

It had been an eye-opening week. Working with the girls had made her realise how much need there was out there, and how many young women could do with a compassionate ear and solid guidance from someone who understood their challenges. In the three one-on-ones based off her first talk, she'd heard about self-harm, eating disorders, difficult home lives and peer pressure, and even one girl who was pregnant and desperately afraid to the point that she was contemplating abortion.

Marta had tried not to let her horror show and counselled the girl as best she could, remembering six years earlier when she'd been in the same position herself, frightened and seemingly alone. Now she knew she'd never truly been alone, and these girls weren't either, even if they didn't know it. As she drove, she prayed for them, knowing that if they could be led in the right way, they could find true freedom, just as she herself had.

She picked Angel up and drove home. A large envelope was poking out of the letterbox. Her breath caught in her throat. Acting on Paul's advice, she'd ordered her mother's birth certificate, but surely it wouldn't be here so soon? She took the envelope and opened it to find that it was, in fact, the certificate. Her heart pounded as she unfolded it and scanned the information.

Her grandmother's name was Maria and her grandfather was Donald, and their address at the time of her mother's birth was in Melbourne, not too far from where Marta herself had grown up with Liza. She tried not to get too excited, reminding herself that the likelihood of her grandparents being at the same address was slim. Still, at least it was somewhere to start, and there might be a forwarding address, if nothing else.

Marta slipped the certificate safely in a drawer and then got on with helping Angel with her homework and making dinner.

Then she bathed her and got her into her pyjamas just before Heidi arrived to babysit.

She greeted Marta and hugged her warmly. "We're so glad Paul has finally asked you out! What are you wearing?"

"I don't know. A long skirt as usual, I guess."

Heidi tutted. "Marta, it's a *date*. What about those nice white jeans you have and that lemon top I gave you last year? The one you've never worn out, but you look absolutely adorable in?"

Marta opened her mouth to protest then gave up as Heidi bounced up the stairs to her bedroom to go through her wardrobe.

Heidi was right, she reflected a little while later as she turned one way and then the other in front of the mirror. She did look nice. She'd teamed the outfit with a pair of wedges with a small heel and she looked summery and pretty. Heidi had done her hair and make-up and she looked cute, with her eyes a little more sultry than usual. "Thanks, Heidi."

"See? What would you do without me?" Heidi grinned, and then clapped her hands in excitement as the doorbell rang. "That will be your date."

Marta breathed deeply, willing herself to be calm as she walked downstairs and opened the door. Paul stood in the entrance with a bunch of flowers that he held out to her. Marta stared at them for a moment, flustered.

"They're flowers," he said, looking bemused. "They don't bite."

Marta felt her cheeks colour. "Thank you. I'll put them in water," she said, taking them from him.

Behind her, Heidi appeared. "Hi Paul. I'll take those," her

friend said chirpily, taking the flowers from Marta and all but pushing her out the door.

As she walked to the car, Marta felt awkward. "Sorry. It's just that...no one has ever bought me flowers before."

"Then I'm glad I was the first," Paul said, holding the passenger door open for her.

As they drove to the cinema, Marta tugged a piece of hair and wrapped it around her finger, feeling self-conscious sitting beside him. She should be used to spending time with Paul by now, but tonight the context was completely different. They were on a *date*. The first proper date she'd really been on. Steve had never taken her out. Marta realised how many simple experiences she'd missed out on when they got to the cinema and started ordering popcorn and choosing pick 'n' mix. She felt herself unwinding—this was fun.

The film they'd chosen was a new historical drama which had amazing reviews. However, half an hour in it became apparent the reviews weren't justified.

Marta and Paul exchanged glances. "This is terrible," he whispered. "Shall we go and eat instead?"

She giggled. "Let's give it a little longer. It mightn't have gotten going yet."

Twenty minutes later they stood outside the cinema, having sneaked out of the film. "There's a nice Italian place up the road," Paul suggested.

"Sounds good."

As they walked, he cleared his throat as though he was readying himself to say something. Marta looked at him as he asked, "Would you mind if I hold your hand?"

She bit her lip, thinking what a gentleman he was, as flutters of nerves tingled in her stomach. "I'd like that," she said.

He slipped his hand around hers, holding it as they walked. Marta felt as though she didn't dare breathe.

Once seated in the restaurant, they placed their orders, and then she told him about her mother's birth certificate. "Of course," she concluded, "my grandparents probably haven't lived there for years. But it's worth a try. I'm thinking of driving down tomorrow."

Paul groaned. "I'd offer to come with you but I've got a seminar this weekend."

Marta shook her head. "It's okay. I'll have Angel, so I'll take her to the Sea Life Centre and then try the address on the way back. Keep it casual. I'll see who opens the door and see if I can get a forwarding address. I'm going to be a lot more careful this time."

Paul nodded thoughtfully. "I know last weekend was a real blow for you. I'll have my phone on, though, so call me if you need anything, okay?"

She smiled. "Thank you," she said sincerely. "Honestly, you've been so supportive."

After they finished their meal, they walked back to the car arm in arm. Marta was amazed at how relaxed she felt in his company. "Thank you for tonight. I've really enjoyed myself," she told him as they reached the passenger side.

He unlocked the car and then turned to her, an expression she couldn't quite place on his face as his eyes gazed steadily into hers. "Marta, I'd really like to kiss you. May I?"

She inhaled sharply but knew instantly what her answer would be. "Yes," she whispered, her heart pounding as he leaned forward and slipped an arm around her waist and softly brushed his lips across hers. It was a sweet rather than a passionate kiss, but even so, a shudder of joy ran through her. His touch felt both incredibly new and yet also somehow oddly familiar. As though they should always have been together.

As they pulled apart, they stared at each other and a current passed between them. Despite her fears, Marta knew that whatever was happening between her and Paul felt inescapably *right*.

He grinned, breaking the tension, as he opened the door for her. On the ride home, when he reached to change gear, he briefly squeezed her hand again, and she didn't feel nervous at all. He gave her a lingering kiss on the cheek before he dropped her off and made her promise to call him the next evening to tell him how things went in Melbourne.

She had a giddy smile on her face as she let herself in, which told Heidi all she needed to know.

"I take it you had a good time, then?"

"Well, the film was rubbish, so we ended up sneaking out."

Heidi rolled her eyes. "I don't care about the film. How were things with Paul?"

Marta gave a dreamy smile as she wrapped her arms around herself. "It was lovely. Really lovely. I like him a lot, Heidi."

Her friend nodded. "I can see that." She laughed. "You look like a love-struck teenager." Her expression softened as she continued. "Enjoy it, Marta. He's a good man, and you deserve that in your life."

Marta smiled at her friend, and for the first time in a long time, she dared to believe that maybe there was love out there for her after all.

She prayed that night for God to watch over her and Angel the next day on their trip to Melbourne, and for Him to watch over Paul. Then she went to sleep with a smile and the memory of Paul's kiss on her lips.

CHAPTER 12

Marta followed the signs for Coburg, the Melbourne suburb where her grandparents had lived when her mother was born. Her pulse raced as she approached the location. Angel sat in the back, reading her Sea Life brochure, blissfully unaware of the turmoil raging in her mother's heart. They'd left early that morning and gone to the Sea Life Centre in Melbourne, which Angel had loved. They'd had lunch there before driving to Coburg, and at first Marta had felt fine, even optimistic about finding her family. She'd spent the previous night and some time this morning praying for strength, and up until five minutes ago had felt strong and confident. Now the doubts were starting to settle.

What if they'd moved away years ago and left no address? Or what if they'd died? She tried to remind herself that whatever the outcome, she would be all right as long as she trusted God to guide her.

Punctuating her nerves were flutters of excitement at the

memory of her date with Paul last night. She guessed the kiss meant they were now officially dating, and after so many years of telling herself she would never trust another man and was happy to remain single, she was amazed at how at ease she felt with that idea. Surely, after such an amazing turn of events, nothing about today could go wrong.

It wasn't helping, she knew, that Coburg wasn't far from the area she'd lived in with Steve. In fact, she'd driven through there on her way and wondered if that had triggered her sudden bout of anxiety. Although she'd been too focused on finding her grandparents to fully register the fact that she'd been only a few streets away from their old apartment, she wondered now if her subconscious had been only too aware, causing the memory of old trauma to flare up. The fact that she had Angel with her made her even more jittery.

She pulled up outside the address she'd been looking for and bowed her head, saying a quick prayer to calm her nerves. Then she glanced at Angel in the rear view. "Sweetie, I'm just going to knock on that door right there. I have to give a message for someone."

"Okay, Mummy," Angel said, not bothering to look up from her brochure. Marta got out, locked the doors and strode purposefully up the short path, taking in the exterior of the house as she did so. It was a small detached property with white wooden slats and had been kept in good condition. The front lawn was neatly trimmed and pretty nets hung at the windows. Whoever lived here now obviously cared for the property.

Marta took a deep breath and knocked on the door. The

nets twitched and then a shadow appeared behind the frosted glass.

As an elderly woman opened the door, Marta couldn't help but gasp. Apart from the grey hair, it was like looking at an older version of Liza Rodriguez. There could be no doubt about it, this was her grandmother.

Marta swallowed, trying not to show her excitement as the woman narrowed her eyes suspiciously at her. "Can I help you?" she asked. Even her voice reminded Marta of her mother's.

"Yes, err, maybe," Marta stammered. She paused and took another breath, trying to collect herself and get a handle on her emotions as the woman raised a brow at her. There could be no mistaking it, she was the same build and colouring as Liza had been, with the same flashing dark eyes. The grey hair and stooped posture couldn't hide the resemblance—she could even see Angel in her. Marta realised that meant that she, too, must look like the woman standing before her. As Maria studied her with squinted eyes, Marta was sure she caught a flash of recognition in the older woman's face.

"My name is Marta Rodriguez," she said softly, "and I'm looking for my grandparents, Maria and Donald Rodriguez. This was listed as their address years ago, when my mother Liza was born."

The woman's face went suddenly blank and her expression chilled, but Marta knew she hadn't imagined the look in her eyes when she'd mentioned the names of her family. A furrowed brow and pinched lips showed a depth of pain.

But now she simply glared at her and began shutting the door. "I have no idea who you're talking about. Sorry."

"Wait!" Marta exclaimed, desperation in her voice. "Do you...not even have a forwarding address?"

"I said I can't help you," the woman said, and shut the door firmly in Marta's face.

Marta looked about helplessly, utterly crushed. She knocked on the door again but this time there was no answer. *Now what?* There was no doubting the resemblance or the woman's reaction, but Marta couldn't force her to acknowledge her. At a loss, she retreated down the path.

In the garden next door, an elderly man was pruning the hedge. On a whim, she approached him and smiled. "Hi," she called out. "How long have you lived next door to Mrs. Rodriguez?"

The old man gave her a toothless grin as he straightened. "Oh, nearly fifty years now, love. We've both been here since these houses were new. Oldest residents on the street."

She had her proof. The woman at the door was, without a shadow of a doubt, Maria Rodriguez. Liza's mother. Her grandmother.

She went to the car and scrambled around in the centre console for a pen and paper. She scribbled down her name, address and telephone number and went back up the path to Maria's front door. Figuring it was pointless to try knocking again, she slid the paper through the door, said a quick prayer and hurried back to the car.

Only after she'd driven away from the street did she realise her hands were shaking.

She reflected as she drove, how in many ways the visit had been a success. She hadn't exactly been welcomed—the complete opposite, in fact—but she'd found her grandparents and had made contact. She had family, after all, and they were alive, and she knew where they lived.

Somehow the knowledge made her feel more anchored in the world. Maybe Maria wasn't ready to talk to her for reasons Marta didn't yet understand, but she had Marta's details now. Marta knew she had to leave the rest in God's hands and trust that whatever happened was exactly what was meant to. After all, she didn't believe for one minute that God had led her all this way for nothing to come of it. The thought settled her nerves, leaving her with a quiet sense of what would be, would be. She glanced at her daughter's beautiful face in the rear view and felt a rush of love and overwhelming gratitude for her.

Even as she drove back through her and Steve's old area, Marta retained the sense of calm. Steve had probably moved years ago, she told herself, and besides, she was determined not to let that particular part of her past haunt her anymore.

"Mummy?" Angel said in a plaintive voice as they approached a small shop with a few tables outside. "Can we please get a drink? I'm sooo thirsty."

Marta hesitated, unwilling to stop in an area that held so many memories. But it was hot, and Angel needed to be kept hydrated in this weather. "Okay, sweetie. Let's grab a drink and then we'll head home. It's been a long day."

The afternoon sun was still high in the sky as she pulled up and got out, slipping on her sunglasses and helping Angel out of the back seat. They walked to the shop hand in hand and Marta ordered them both an iced drink. As she took the drinks and turned around, she looked across the far side of the street and froze.

A pick-up truck that looked like Steve's had pulled up on

the opposite side of the road. She was sure it was his. How many trucks had a skull and crossbones on the door? So, he did still live around here. She ushered Angel back into the car, panic welling as she closed the door and hurried around to her own side with her heart hammering. As she sat behind the wheel, she looked in her side mirror and stiffened. She slid down into the seat as the unmistakable figure of Steve got out of the pick-up.

As far as she could tell from where she was, he hadn't changed much. It looked like he'd gained some weight but it was unmistakably him. The scowl on his face triggered a flashback of him towering over her, his hand raised, and she realised she was shaking. Pulling herself together before either Angel noticed something was wrong or Steve noticed her, she started the engine.

Then someone else got out of the other side of the pick-up. A young woman with long mousy hair tied in a ponytail.

She was heavily pregnant.

Steve barked something at her as he walked along the footpath. The girl hurried to catch up with him, fear etched on her face. As they got closer, Marta could see that despite her pregnancy, she was desperately thin and her face looked pinched and hollow. It could be Marta herself, years ago.

She felt sick. Hitting the pedal, she pulled away quickly and sped down the road.

"Are you okay, Mummy?"

Marta swallowed hard. "Yes, darling. I just want to get home. I'm really tired after our day out."

"Me too," Angel said with a yawn.

Marta gripped the steering wheel, her stomach churning as

she processed what had just happened. It had been the first time she'd laid eyes on Steve since he'd attacked her when she was heavily pregnant with Angel, so to see him so close after all this time had shaken her up enough...but to see him with that pregnant girl... She wondered if Steve was abusing her too. She thought of his scowl and the way he'd snapped at the girl, and the downcast look on her face, and Marta knew in her gut that Steve was mistreating this slip of a girl just as he'd mistreated her.

It's not your problem, Marta tried to tell herself, *and there's nothing you can do.* But the wretched look on the girl's face haunted her. She was in danger, Marta was sure of it.

After twenty minutes she pulled over. An idea was forming in her mind. She wasn't far from Daisy's homeless shelter. Quickly making her decision, she swung the car around and pointed it in the direction of the shelter.

CHAPTER 13

Daisy was thrilled to see Marta and Angel and invited them to stay the night. The afternoon passed pleasantly and over the course of several hours, Marta told Daisy all that had been happening in her life, including her new relationship with Paul and her quest to find her family. She didn't tell Daisy, however, that she'd seen Steve and held grave fears for the girl he was now with. That bit of information she kept to herself.

After lying awake all night thinking about the girl, Marta made up her mind. She had to try to help her. She'd never forgive herself if she didn't and later discovered something bad had happened.

It was awkward telling Daisy she needed to visit an old friend instead of attending church. Daisy narrowed her eyes but didn't push for information when Marta asked if she would mind taking Angel to church with her.

After the pair left, Marta set off on her mission, although

guilt gnawed at her insides over keeping her plans secret not only from Daisy, but Paul as well. When they'd talked on the phone the night before, she didn't mention it to him. If she had, she was sure he'd advise her not to go. Maybe she was being foolhardy, but she had a deep inner conviction that this was something she had to do.

Twenty minutes later, with her heart beating in her throat, Marta pulled up outside the shop where she and Angel had sat outside the day before, bought a coffee, and sat nervously at a table facing the other side of the road.

There was no sign of Steve's pick-up. She was both relieved and disappointed, but now that she was here, she realised with dismay that she had no real plan for what to do next. She didn't know Steve's exact address, and even if she did, could she knock on the door and risk coming face to face with him? *How was she supposed to find the girl and then arrange to speak with her?* She really hadn't thought this through properly.

She took a deep breath. She had to trust her intuition. Although what she was doing could be dangerous and flew in the face of common sense, she felt strongly that the Lord had placed her in this situation for a reason.

She sat there long enough for her coffee to grow cold and was about to give up when a pregnant woman emerged from the apartment building across the road dragging a bin bag over the grass to the large communal bins.

Marta straightened. It was her. The young woman she'd seen yesterday. It had to be her. Assuming she was alone since Steve's truck wasn't there, Marta stood and hurried across the road, calling out to her before she disappeared inside.

She made a mental note of which number the girl was

about to enter. "Hey! Excuse me," Marta called, jogging up to her.

The girl glanced around furtively. Up close, Marta could see how young she was, probably no older than eighteen, and so thin. She also had a faded bruise on her cheekbone. Marta felt sick.

The girl looked at her warily. "Can I help you?"

"Hi, yes," Marta said, taking some short breaths. "Have you got a minute to talk? It's about Steve."

The girl shrunk back, her shoulders drawing together. "What…what about him?" Wariness tinged her voice.

Marta smiled and tried to look as sympathetic and non-threatening as possible even though her insides churned with anxiety. "It's okay," she said soothingly. "I was driving past here yesterday and saw you with him—and heard the way he spoke to you."

"I don't know what you mean," the girl snapped and went to turn away, but not before Marta saw the fear in her eyes.

Marta put a hand on her arm, and although her touch was light, the way the girl immediately flinched told Marta all she needed to know. "I used to be with him," she said, talking quickly, "and he was abusive to me, too. When I saw you yesterday, I knew I couldn't ignore the fact that he's hurting someone else. Especially in your condition."

The girl stared at her but didn't move away.

Encouraged, Marta continued. "Trust me, I know how hard it is and that you're probably really scared right now, but you *can* get away from him. I'd like to help, if you'd let me. I got away, and now I work with other women fleeing abusive men. I can help."

Marta saw the flare of hope in the girl's eyes. Then they dimmed and clouded over. Marta knew that look—complete and utter despair.

"If I tried to get away, he'd kill me," the girl whispered.

Marta felt as though her heart would break. The girl looked incredibly fragile, and apart from her bulging stomach, she was unhealthily thin. "We can keep you safe," she promised. "He never has to hurt you again."

The girl burst into tears and Marta went to embrace her, but she pushed her away, shaking her head. "You have to go," she said between sobs. "He'll be back any minute. Please."

"Okay." Marta nodded quickly. "But can I at least give you my number?"

The girl shook her head. "He might find it. Tell me and I'll remember it."

Marta said her number and asked her to repeat it twice. Then as the girl rushed away, she said, "What's your name? I'm Marta."

"Piper," the girl whispered before disappearing behind a swinging door.

Marta hurried back to her car and drove off, the girl's panic having ignited her own. Just before she turned out of the street, in her rear-view mirror she saw Steve's pick-up entering it at the other end and realised how close she'd been to bumping into him. Her hands trembled on the wheel as she headed back to Daisy's, praying all the way for Piper and her unborn baby.

Daisy and Angel were back from church and were preparing lunch when she arrived. Marta plastered on a smile, but Daisy eyed her with concern when she walked in.

"Has something happened? You look awfully pale."

"I'm fine," Marta replied, hugging Angel and not meeting Daisy's gaze. After lunch, she put the television on for Angel and quickly told Daisy what had happened. She had to tell someone. The girl's frightened eyes were haunting her.

When Marta said she'd seen Steve, Daisy gasped and her hand flew to her mouth. When she told her about Piper, Daisy shook her head, her eyes narrowing. "That man! Still up to his old tricks, then."

"I have to help her," Marta said wretchedly.

Daisy sighed, her shoulders dropping. "I understand why you feel like that. God knows, so do I." She reached out her hand. "But Marta, you can't go back. He's dangerous. You've given the girl your number. All you can do is wait and see if she calls."

She nodded. Daisy was right, but she desperately wanted to do something. She fell quiet as Angel stood and asked when they were leaving.

"Now, sweetheart." They hugged and said their goodbyes, although Marta could see that Daisy was now trying to hide her concern. "Be careful," she mouthed as Marta pulled away, and then blew Angel a kiss.

Angel fell asleep in the car on the way home leaving Marta alone with her thoughts. Seeing Steve had stirred so much inner conflict and she felt jittery and fragile herself and knew she was identifying with Piper. Coming face to face with the girl had been like confronting her old self, and now all the memories and pain flooded back like it was yesterday.

Recalling the passage about putting on the armour of God, she prayed for peace and protection, and although that fortified her somewhat and her immediate panic subsided, she felt unsettled all the way home.

By the time she got back to Salford it was late afternoon and she knew Paul would be on his way back from the conference. She called him, feeling a rush of warmth at the sound of his voice.

"Hey. How was your day?" she asked. She tried to pay attention as he told her about his day at the conference, but her thoughts kept returning to Piper.

It seemed that even over the phone, Paul sensed something was worrying her. "What's wrong, Marta?" he asked softly.

The story tumbled out of her.

Paul was silent for a moment before he replied. "I know you want to help and I completely understand why," he said warily. "But you must be careful, Marta. You can't go rushing in. He's a dangerous man, and if she's not ready to leave, you know yourself you can't make her."

"I know," she whispered. She remembered all too keenly what it felt like to be trapped in such a situation out of sheer fear. "I know I've done all I can for now. I just have to hope she calls, or that I've at least planted a seed of hope."

"Pray for her," Paul advised gently. "Our prayers are more powerful than we know."

He was right. Prayer was the only thing that would help the girl now. They arranged to meet after work at the pool the next day, as Angel had another class, and said goodbye. As she put the phone down, tiredness washed over her.

She ran a bath for Angel and put dinner on, trying to distract herself by thinking about the week ahead. It was going to be another busy one. She had another talk to do the next day and more girls to see, and she was looking forward to spending time with Paul. She had to put Piper to the back of her mind.

And yet, despite her resolve, thoughts of the girl plagued her all night.

CHAPTER 14

Marta closed her eyes as she sank into the pool, feeling the cool water wash over her. She was looking forward to a good swim. It had been an emotional day. The morning's talk had gone well, and in fact, she thought she'd reached more girls than ever and her speech had been particularly emotive. She was sure, however, that was because Piper had been on her mind the whole time, and her concern for the girl had lent her talk a raw emotion her audience had picked up on. Although that might have been a good thing for the girls who were listening to her, Marta knew she had to find a way to relax and let go of some of the tension. She was full of nervous energy and felt like a coiled spring.

She heard a splash. Opening her eyes, she smiled. Paul had dived into the lane next to her.

The tenderness in his eyes offered her some comfort. "Ready for some laps?" he asked.

"You bet," she said with a grin.

As they swam, Marta put all that pent-up energy to good use, keeping up with Paul lap after lap, her lean body slicing through the water. On the final lap she beat him by just a smidgeon, and she turned to him triumphantly, out of breath from exertion.

"You were on fire today," he remarked afterwards as they sat on the benches at the nearby park while Angel played on the swings.

Marta nodded. "I've had so much emotion pent up inside me today. After the talk, and yesterday, and seeing my grandmother."

After the drama with Piper, Marta had almost forgotten that she'd actually managed to find her grandmother, even if Mrs. Rodriguez had been decidedly less than welcoming.

"Are you going to see her again?" Paul asked.

Marta shrugged. "I don't know. I want to—I have so many questions to ask. But I don't want to upset her by turning up on her doorstep unannounced again. She must have had her reasons for pretending not to know who I was." Marta winced as she felt the sting of rejection once more. Paul took her hand in his. "I suppose I just have to wait and see if she calls," she said sadly.

Paul squeezed her hand. "You could write a letter," he suggested. "That isn't too intrusive and will also give you a chance to say the things you want to, and give her time to think about how or whether to reply."

Marta gave a half-smile. "That's a good idea. Thank you." She released a heavy sigh. "I feel so helpless at the minute. Everything is out of my control…whether my grandmother calls, whether or not Piper calls, whether I actually manage to get through to any of these girls..." Her voice trailed off. She didn't want to say but was thinking, that her fledgling relationship with Paul, as wonderful as it was, also made her anxious. It was all so much to deal with.

Paul seemed to have read her mind. "I know you have a lot going on right now," he said softly. "If you need me to take a step back..."

She blinked and shook her head. "No! I'm really happy we're getting to know each other," she said honestly, but she felt her face blush under his steady gaze. "This is just all new for me. I thought I'd be alone forever, after Steve."

Paul nodded. "I understand. I mean, I haven't been through the things you've been through, but after my parents died, I closed part of myself off to love—until you came along." His eyes brimmed with tenderness and passion. "I know we have to take things slowly," he said softly, massaging her hand with his thumb, "but I want you to know you mean a lot to me, Marta. And I'm here for you."

"Thank you," she whispered, almost unable to speak. "I...I feel the same."

They sat together in silence, holding hands until Paul offered to pray with her. Marta nodded, and they clasped hands and prayed together on the bench where they sat.

"Father God, Lord of all," Paul began, "I pray that You'll be with Marta this week. Guide her path and the steps she takes towards You. Help her remember that she's never alone and that You're always with her, and help her to look to You for her rest and refuge. Calm her spirit, Lord, and send Your healing balm, lend her Your wisdom and Your strength, and help her surrender and trust in You. In Your Son's precious name. Amen."

"Amen," Marta echoed quietly, and then continued. "Lord, thank You for Your continued presence and guidance. Help me to walk in Your footsteps and follow Your way and not be distracted by my own fears and desires. Keep watch over Piper, and over my grandmother, and if they don't know You already, Lord, I pray that they'll find grace and healing in You. Amen."

She opened her eyes and realised her cheeks were damp with tears.

Paul let go of her hands, and lifting his own to her cheeks, wiped away her tears.

Marta smiled and silently thanked God for bringing Paul into her life. She was so blessed.

Angel ran over to the bench where they were sitting and Marta turned her attention to her daughter, her cheeks tingling where Paul had just touched her.

THAT NIGHT, Marta wrote her grandmother a letter which she then posted the next morning, uttering a prayer as she did so. She'd kept it short and polite, reassuring Mrs. Rodriguez that she simply wanted an opportunity to get to know her family and her own background. She told her that she had a daughter, was a Christian, and worked at the local women's refuge. She also included a small photo of herself and Angel. She finished by saying she would leave it to her to decide whether to make further contact or not, but that she would be thinking of her. Then she tried to do as Paul had prayed and leave the outcome with God.

As hard as she tried not to, she found herself constantly checking her phone every day that week, sighing in frustration when there were no calls from either her grandmother or Piper. Piper's predicament played on her mind. Work was as busy as usual but even that couldn't distract her for long. In the end, towards the end of the week, she left her phone at home during the day so she couldn't be tempted to keep checking it while at work.

On Friday afternoon, Vanessa insisted she book a few days off the following week. "You've been working really hard, Marta, and now that you're so in demand for talks and one-on-one sessions, you'll be really busy next month too. But the beginning of next week is quiet. Please take some days off. You're owed it. I don't want you burning out."

In the end Marta agreed, although she had no idea what she'd do with herself. Angel would be at school and Paul at work. She was a doer and had no idea what to do with 'down-time' as Amy would call it.

Although she still had to force herself not to keep checking her phone, the weekend was much more relaxed. On Saturday, she and Paul took Angel to a play area on the outskirts of Salford, and on Sunday they all went to church together and then to Amy and Angus' for lunch. Angus and Paul got on well, and Amy was overjoyed that he and Marta were now dating.

She too was concerned when Marta told her about Piper. "You can't go rushing in there trying to save her," Amy admonished. "Paul's right. Let God handle this."

"But don't you think sometimes God wants us to act on His behalf?"

"Most definitely." Amy smiled. "But if that's the case, you'll sense it, won't you? You know when you're running on your own will, Marta Rodriguez."

Marta chuckled. Her friend was right. She'd always had a tendency to be headstrong and knew she had to wait on the Lord, the One who always delivered on His promises. But it was hard. So hard.

That night, however, Marta felt prompted to do a little more research. She felt strongly that there was a reason her grandmother had reacted the way she had. She typed her grandparents' names into Google...and then sat back in horror at the headline that popped up on the screen.

Melbourne Man Jailed for Murder of Daughter's Lover

Holding her breath, Marta clicked on the link and read down the page, letting her breath out in a slow, shocked exhale. No wonder her grandmother had reacted the way she had.

Donald Rodriguez, her grandfather, had been convicted in 1995—the year after Marta was born—for killing David Harris and had been sentenced to fifteen years in prison.

Unable to read on as she struggled to process what she had already read, she felt the blood pounding in her ears. The truth hit her like a block of ice.

Her grandfather had killed her father.

Her search for her father had been fruitless all along because he was dead. At the hands of her own family. Now it all made sense why her mother had barely spoken of either Marta's father or her own parents. But why? Why would Donald have killed David? The only clue the article gave was that Donald had been convicted of manslaughter rather than murder, so perhaps he hadn't meant to kill him. But a sentence of fifteen years indicated that it was more than just an accident.

She had to know the truth. Why hadn't she thought to research her family before, rather than just look for addresses? But then, who would ever have expected to discover something like this? Where was her grandfather now? Did he still live in the house with her grandmother? Had he been there the other day? He should have gotten out in 2010 if the article was right about his sentence. She typed in his name and release date and waited to see if anything came up.

It did, and brought with it another shock that left Marta reeling.

Donald, too, was dead. He'd died of pneumonia in prison just a few years before he was due to be released. Marta covered her face with her hands and realised she was blinking back tears. This was worse than she'd thought. She'd expected to find that her father hadn't been a good man, or worse, but...not this.

The only remaining member of her family, she realised, was her grandmother. And she hadn't wanted to acknowledge her. Given that history, Marta understood that her sudden visit must have dragged up so many painful memories for Maria Rodriguez.

With sudden clarity, she knew she had to see her again. Although it had been her sincere intention to leave it in the other woman's hands, Marta knew she needed the truth about what had happened to her family. There was no way she could simply walk away from this.

As a plan started to form, she was grateful to have been given a day off work the following day. Also, that Amy was picking Angel up from school to take her back for a play date with Archie, something they took in turns doing every fortnight or so. Marta would have plenty of time to drive to Melbourne after she dropped Angel at school, visit her grandmother and be back in time to pick her daughter up from Amy's.

She wondered if she should tell Amy her plans but decided against it. She wanted to keep this to herself until she had a better idea of the full story. When Paul phoned to say goodnight, she didn't even mention it to him and felt guilty once again at keeping secrets from him. But she was sure that both he and Amy would either try to talk her out of it or insist on going with her. And as much as she knew how headstrong and willful she could be, sometimes to her own detriment, and that Paul would no doubt remind her to trust God, she didn't feel her decision was wrong. In fact, the more she prayed on it that night and asked God for guidance, allowing her heart to be open to His will, the more she was certain she needed to go and see her grandmother. Alone.

THE NEXT DAY, Marta pulled up outside Maria's house and took a deep breath. Centring herself, she closed her eyes and prayed.

Dear Lord, let all be according to Your will. Help Maria to open her heart to me, and keep me strong and steadfast, no matter what I should find out today about my family. Because ultimately, You are my Father, and You love me and Angel as no other. Help me to remember that. In Jesus' precious name. Amen.

Opening her eyes, she stepped out of the car and strode to

Maria's front door. She tapped on it lightly, her heart pounding. When there was no answer, she knocked a little louder.

A few moments later her grandmother appeared behind the glass. She opened the door just enough to peek through, and before she could shut it on her, Marta said quickly, "I'm sorry to bother you. I know I said I'd leave it up to you, but I've only just found out what happened to my father and I need to know the truth. Please?"

Her grandmother stared at her. There was no hostility in her gaze, only sadness. She gave Marta a tired smile. "It's funny, but I'd made up my mind to call you today." She opened the door wider. "Come in."

Marta followed her into a small living room. The house was basic and sparse, and she guessed her grandmother was not very well off, but it was tidy and clean and obviously loved. With a jolt, Marta saw that her grandmother had placed the photograph of herself and Angel on the fireplace.

"You put our picture up," she said softly.

Her grandmother nodded. "Yes. Sit down, Marta." She waved her into a chair and they sat opposite each other. Maria stared into the distance for a few moments before she focused her gaze on Marta, her eyes moist.

"You look so much like your mother. That was what shocked me when I opened the door to you when you were here before. The last time I saw your mother...well it wasn't good. I'm ashamed to say I hated her for what happened to Donald. And after she disappeared, for taking you away from me."

"Did you know me?" Marta leaned forward, her mind reeling. She'd assumed she'd never met her grandmother before.

"The last time I saw you, you were eight months old." A wistful smile creased her wrinkled face. "Such a bonny little thing." Her expression grew sad. "I tried to find you both, but Liza didn't want to be found. I didn't even hear about her death until a year after she died. I made enquiries about you, but you'd disappeared into the care system and no one would tell me anything." Maria shook her head sadly, tears welling in her eyes. "I always worried about you. I'm sorry I let you down."

Marta shook her head vehemently. "It wasn't your fault," she said, struggling to fight back her own tears. She knew she would never be able to explain just how much it meant to her to know that her grandmother had looked for her and had thought about her.

"When I saw you at the door," Maria continued, "I panicked. I resigned myself years ago to never knowing what happened to you. And then you turned up looking so much like your mother...I didn't know what to do. I sat staring at your number for days, and then your letter arrived and I've read it over and over. I finally plucked up the courage to call you today, and yet here you are. I didn't know how much you knew, you see. Or what Liza had told you."

"She never told me anything," Marta said with a sigh. Briefly she described her mother's silence on the subject of her family and her battle with alcohol.

Maria reached for the cross hanging around her neck and closed her eyes. Finally, when she reopened them, she said quietly, "I should start at the beginning."

Marta sat back in the chair, her heart beating in her throat. She was about to discover the truth about her family.

"Liza was our only child," her grandmother began. "I had complications when she was born and so we could never have any more. Perhaps we doted on her too much, I don't know. But she was a happy girl. Strong willed and defiant, certainly, but mostly a delight. Then she started to go off the rails a little once she went to college. Skipping class, staying out all night. We were at our wits end. We knew it had to be a man, and so we confronted her, told her to bring him home, get it out in the open. Then she brought David home." At the hard edge that sounded in her grandmother's voice, it was obvious she hadn't approved of Marta's father from the very beginning.

"We'd heard of him, you see. Donald had heard talk at work and down at the pub. He was a bad sort, into crime and drugs and who knows what else. A lot older than your mother. He came swaggering in here to meet us with this smirk on his face...and the minute I laid eyes on him I knew he was going to be Liza's downfall. But she couldn't see it. And the more we tried to keep her away from him, the more she ran towards him. Then she told us she was pregnant." Maria gave a heavy sigh and went quiet.

"What happened then?" Marta whispered, although part of her wondered if she really wanted to know.

"Donald threw her out. He was furious. Hurt, too, but he was a stubborn man and wouldn't admit that. I kept in touch with Liza, though. She was my daughter, and she was having my grandchild, but it was difficult because David did everything he could to keep her away and turn her against us. He was horrible to her, got her on the drink, but he seemed to have some kind of spell over her."

Marta nodded, thinking of Steve. As she'd suspected, her

father had been just like him. She felt a stab of grief for her mother, and for the woman in front of her whose whole life had been ripped apart.

"Then she had you, and oh, you were such a delight. And she loved you, your mother. Whatever she became, the day you were born was the happiest of her life."

Unbidden tears rolled down Marta's cheeks.

"But David became more and more brutal. I was so worried about you both. One night I begged Donald to do something, to try and get you both away. So what happened was my fault, really. We went around to the place they were living and tried to talk sense into your mother, but David turned up and started yelling. He grabbed your mother by the arm—she was holding you. Donald saw red."

Marta held her breath, sensing what was about to come next.

"He killed David. He didn't mean to. He only used his fists, but Donald was a boxer in his youth, you see, and a very good one. He won all the county fairs. He knocked David out and he never got up again. Donald was arrested and your mother disappeared. I never saw her—or you—again. I tried, for years, and always thought she would turn up one day, but she never did..." Maria's voice trailed away, and Marta leaned over and grabbed her hands.

"It wasn't your fault," she said urgently. "You mustn't blame yourself for any of it."

Maria shook her head. "How could I not? I was her mother. I waited for Donald, of course, and went to see him every month. I was so looking forward to him getting out of prison so we could resume some kind of life again, but then he grew ill."

Both Marta and her grandmother were crying now.

"Please," Maria said quietly, "Tell me that things are better for you."

Marta wondered how much to tell her and decided it was important to be honest. "I was put into care after Mum died. It was hard. I felt so unwanted. Then I met an older man, and by the sound of things, he was exactly like my father. But," she hastened to continue as she saw the pain in her grandmother's eyes, "I escaped from him when I was seventeen. He's Angel's father but he's never seen her. I work as a women's support officer now, and I've met someone."

"Is he nice?"

Marta couldn't help but smile. "He's wonderful. In fact, he's a school chaplain. It's early days, but I have a lot of hope for the future."

Her grandmother smiled. "I'd love to hear more about him, and your work, and…and Angel? Is that your daughter's name?" she asked tentatively.

A wave of fondness towards her grandmother flowed through Marta. Her grandmother's story—and her own—were so sad, yet she had finally found what was left of her family and learned the truth, even if it was terrible. "Of course. And yes. Her name is Angel."

Maria made more tea and cut some cake, and Marta stayed for a while, telling her all about Angel and how well she was doing, and her work at the refuge and the school talks, and how she met Paul. When she stood to leave, explaining she had to get back for Angel, they both looked at each other awkwardly, neither wanting to leave the other, now that they'd finally found one another.

Marta spoke first. "It would be lovely if we could stay in touch. If you want to, that is. And maybe you and Angel could meet?"

The beaming smile Maria gave her warmed her heart. Marta stepped forward and embraced her grandmother, feeling the frailty of the older woman in her arms and thanking God fervently for bringing them together at last.

She left having arranged to bring Angel on the weekend, and she drove off with joy in her heart, although it was tinged with sadness for her mother and grandfather.

She was surprised to realise that she felt no resentment towards her father, although she was bitterly disappointed. In many ways, however, it felt as though a weight had been lifted. She'd been so scared of meeting him and finding out that he was just like Steve, that as awful as the news had been, at least she would never have to confront him or worry about another potentially abusive relative situation. And she'd found Maria, a blessing so large she almost felt her heart would burst with gratitude. Hearing that Liza had loved her so much as a baby had helped heal some old wounds, too.

It was so tragic, however, that even without knowing what she was doing, her life had so very nearly followed a similar trajectory to her mother's. As she approached the area where Steve lived, she couldn't help but think about Piper. Although she'd managed to break the cycle Liza had begun and get Angel away, there was another woman and child stuck in that very same situation. As Marta drove down the street, she saw that Steve's pick-up wasn't there, but she resolutely kept her eyes on the road, telling herself not to interfere. She'd given Piper her number and that was all she could do.

But then she felt a whispering inside her heart.

Go to her.

Marta slowed the car. This didn't feel like an impulsive urge; this felt like the promptings of the Spirit.

"Really, Lord?" she whispered, and then felt it again.

She needs you. Go to her.

Marta pulled up outside the apartment block and turned off the engine.

CHAPTER 15

Holding her breath, Marta entered the apartment block and knocked on the door that Piper had gone in through before. She waited, tense, ready to make a run for it if Steve happened to answer. After a few minutes, she heard a faint voice from within.

"Who is it?"

It was Piper, and she sounded scared.

"It's Marta," she said quietly through the door. "Are you alone?"

"Yes."

"Are you okay?"

There was silence. It went on long enough that Marta thought Piper was going to ignore her, but then she heard the lock being slid back.

Marta gasped when Piper opened the door. Her left eye was hugely swollen and bruised and there were bruises around her neck.

"Steve did that," Marta said grimly, making a statement rather than asking a question.

Piper nodded and her eyes filled with tears. "I was going to phone you, but Steve smashed my phone up. You have to help me get away," she begged. "I'm frightened that he's going to hurt the baby."

Marta closed her eyes as memories from her own past with Steve flashed into her mind. Praying silently for strength, she opened her eyes and nodded firmly at the girl. "Get some things together and I'll take you to the refuge, unless you have somewhere else to go."

Piper shook her head. "I can't tell my parents. They'll be so ashamed of me."

"How long do we have until Steve comes back?"

She shrugged. "I don't know. But he said he was going to the pub, and that usually means he'll be gone for hours."

Marta took a deep breath of relief and followed Piper inside, helping the girl to pack her bags. The apartment reminded her so much of the one she used to share with Steve that she felt nauseous. Piper had obviously tried to make it clean and nice, but it was shabby and bare. No doubt Steve had sold anything of value she might have had.

Piper had finished packing her bag and they were about to leave when a key turned in the lock. Marta looked at Piper, who was wide-eyed and froze in the spot where she stood, whimpering with fear.

Steve walked in. Motionless, Marta stared at him, her breath catching in her throat. She saw the anger in his eyes and remembered it all too well.

He was glaring at Piper, taking in the bags. Then he looked at Marta. "Who the hell are you?" he spat.

Marta didn't answer. Her heart was pounding with fear.

He peered at her suspiciously, and then she saw his face change as he recognised her.

"Marta?"

"Steve," she said quietly. "I see you haven't changed." She felt a wave of righteous anger that chased away her fear, even when he swore at her.

Then he turned to Piper. "You've been listening to her lies? You were going to leave me?"

He looked crazed, Marta realised, and his pupils were dilated, his eyes darting all around. He was clearly high.

Suddenly he moved towards Piper and backhanded her hard across the face. The girl fell to the floor, clutching her stomach.

Marta jumped in front of Steve as his arm lifted to strike Piper while she lay on the floor.

"Leave her alone!" she screamed.

Steve bellowed with rage and backhanded her too.

Marta went flying but managed to stay on her feet. He stood menacingly over Piper, who was curled up into a ball and moaning.

"I'm not scared of you anymore," Marta said firmly. While she was certainly frightened of what he could do to Piper and her, she wasn't scared of *him*. For the first time she saw him not as a monster, but as a broken and pathetic man.

Piper moaned again. Marta looked down—a puddle had spread around the girl. Her waters had broken. Marta looked at Steve and said, calmly but urgently, hoping she could reason with him, "Steve, she's in labour. You have to call an ambulance."

His lip curled and he snarled. "You do it," he said, and roared with laughter. "You came here wanting to help her, so you help her. You can deliver the baby!" He laughed as though he'd said the funniest thing ever.

Marta reached for the phone in her pocket, but in a flash he'd grabbed her, twisted her arm up and taken her phone, flinging it against the wall. The screen smashed to bits. Then he stood in front of the door, barring the exit and grinning like a maniac. Marta felt her stomach drop.

"Well come on then," he said in a sing-song voice, "get on with it." He nodded towards Piper.

Marta realised that he had gone truly crazy—and was more dangerous than ever.

CHAPTER 16

Paul phoned Marta again and tried to ignore the unease in his stomach when once again her phone went to voice mail. He glanced at the clock. She should have picked Angel up by now. Then he remembered that Angel had gone to Amy's after school.

It's probably nothing, he tried to convince himself, *she's either busy or her phone has died.* But he couldn't shake the feeling that had been creeping up on him all day. In his gut, he just knew something was wrong.

In the end he drove to Amy's. It was nearly dinner time, so surely Marta would be there by now. He'd checked Marta's house on the way, somehow not surprised when she wasn't home. He doubted that she would be at Amy's either, even though he tried to tell himself that he was overreacting. She would think he was daft worrying like this simply because her phone was off. But Paul had learned to trust his instincts, and when he prayed, the inner warnings only got louder, telling him all he needed to know.

Something was wrong.

Amy answered the door, surprised to see him.

"Is Marta here?" he asked.

Amy shook her head slowly. "No. As a matter of fact she's a little late picking Angel up, which is not like her. I just tried to phone her but..."

"Her phone is off," Paul finished.

Amy nodded, biting her lip. "Do you think something has happened?" She let Paul in, ushering him into the kitchen so that Angel didn't see him.

Paul told her how he thought Marta had been on edge all week, worrying about her grandmother and Piper.

Amy shook her head. "She's gone there," she said, her voice so full of certainty that Paul knew she was right. It made perfect sense, given how determined Marta was to do the right thing.

"She could be in danger," he said, a wave of fear coming over him. He couldn't lose her, he suddenly thought, panicking. Not like he had lost his parents. He rested a hand on the wall to steady himself.

Amy picked up her phone. "I'm going to ring the police in Melbourne. Do you know the address where the young woman lives?"

"Marta told me...I think I can remember."

But the police were of little use. Without proof Marta was there or in any danger, they could do nothing other than drive past.

Amy, ever pragmatic, rang Angus on his way home from work. "I need you to go to Melbourne," she said.

Paul listened as Amy filled her husband in, admiring her practical attitude despite the fact that her face was now white with fear.

Amy put the phone down. Despite her bravado, she was holding back tears. "Angus will go with you," she whispered. "It's just like before."

"Before?"

Amy nodded. "When she was pregnant with Angel. Steve lured her back with empty promises. Angus and I went around to where he lived and we found her on the floor, unconscious. Steve had hit her and forced her to take drugs. She was heavily pregnant at the time."

Paul felt a wave of anger building at this Steve who had caused Marta so much pain. Balling his fists, his teeth clenched and all he could think about was hurting him. He closed his eyes and prayed for God to take his anger away and make him useful to Marta instead.

Ten minutes later he was driving with Angus in the passenger seat, heading towards Melbourne, going as fast as he possibly could. Angus kept trying Marta's phone, but it was still off, and Paul felt himself growing more and more panicked.

"Please Lord," he pleaded, "let Marta be okay."

Angus joined in, praying as Paul drove, which helped him to focus his mind somewhat.

By the time they reached their destination, Paul was on his last nerve. He practically ran towards the apartment block with Angus close behind.

"Do you know which one it is?"

"I think she said number three."

Angus pounded on the door. There was no answer, but they both heard someone wailing inside.

"Marta!" Paul hollered, banging on the door.

"Paul!"

"Shut up!" A man's voice cut through the door. Paul and Angus exchanged glances, and then they both launched themselves at the door but it didn't give.

"It's one of those heavy fire doors," Angus said through gritted teeth.

Paul phoned the police, and this time they assured him that they would be there immediately. He only hoped they'd be quick enough. They could still hear the girl—Paul assumed it was Piper—wailing.

"Go away!" the man's voice shouted. "Or I'll kill them both." He laughed maniacally.

Paul felt like his heart was being torn from his chest. He loved Marta, and just when he had found her, he could lose her.

Just like he'd lost his parents. He sighed deeply.

Angus put a comforting hand on his back. "It's going to be okay," he assured. "The police are on their way."

Paul prayed desperately that they wouldn't be too late.

CHAPTER 17

Marta sat with her arms around Piper, holding her as another contraction racked the girl's body. Steve was pacing up and down in front of the door, mumbling to himself, as he had been for the past few hours. Marta felt as though she was in a nightmare, but unfortunately it was all too real.

Still, she kept telling herself, it would be all right in the end. God had guided her there, of that she had no doubt, and so her job right now was to help Piper as best she could. So far Steve hadn't been violent again, although his behaviour was growing increasingly erratic. Marta wondered if he had drug psychosis, or if the drugs had exacerbated an underlying mental health problem. He was even crazier than when she'd been with him; in fact he seemed completely unhinged. She could almost feel sorry for him if it wasn't for the fact that she and Piper were trapped.

When she'd heard Paul's voice on the other side of the door, relief flowed through her, but so far it seemed to have only made things worse. The police had been called and were now outside the apartment, but Steve was refusing to let them in—and had threatened to hurt her and Piper if they broke in. He was holding them hostage, and Marta had no idea where it would all end.

Piper tipped back her head and let out a cry of pain, her hands gripping Marta's so hard that Marta winced.

Steve looked at them wide-eyed. "What's wrong with her?"

"She's having the baby. She's in labour," Marta said slowly and calmly. "You have to let her out, Steve, or both she and the baby could die."

He narrowed his eyes. "You're trying to trick me."

Marta shook her head. "No. Let Piper out so she can go to the hospital, and I'll stay here."

He looked almost childlike. "You promise?"

Marta nodded, swallowing down her fear. Steve really wasn't well, and she suspected that only made him more dangerous. But the most important thing right now was to get Piper and her baby to the hospital.

Steve spoke to the policemen outside the door, telling them that he was going to let Piper out, but he would stay inside with Marta—and if they tried anything, he would kill Marta and himself. Then he hauled both women to their feet and pushed a whimpering Piper towards the door while keeping a tight grip on Marta. As soon as he unbolted the door, he shoved Piper out and rebolted it before the policemen could push through.

Marta closed her eyes and prayed that Piper and the baby would make it. Then, under her breath, she repeated the lines from Ephesians that had helped strengthen her the night before her first talk.

For our struggle is not against flesh and blood, but against the rulers, against the authorities, against the powers of this dark world and against the spiritual forces of evil in the heavenly realms. Therefore put on the full armour of God, so that when the day of evil comes, you may be able to stand your ground, and after you have done everything, to stand. Stand firm then, with the belt of truth buckled around your waist, with the breastplate of righteousness in place, and with your feet fitted with the readiness that comes from the gospel of peace. In addition to all this, take up the shield of faith, with which you can extinguish all the flaming arrows of the evil one. Take the helmet of salvation and the sword of the Spirit, which is the word of God.

"What are you saying?" Steve shook her roughly "Who are you talking to?"

"I'm praying, Steve," she said calmly. "Would you like me to pray for you too?"

He stared at her in shock. "For me?" He laughed bitterly. "God doesn't want you to pray for me, Marta."

She fixed him with a level stare. "It doesn't matter what you've done, Steve," she said with conviction, "God will hear your prayer. It's never too late to change."

His face twisted with emotion and she wondered for a horrible moment if her words had tipped him over the edge. Then, to her amazement, he began to cry. He let go of her arm and sunk to his knees, tears rolling down his cheeks.

Marta crouched next to him. "Lord," she began softly, "open Steve's heart that he may know You love him. Bring him Your peace and Your guidance. May he know that he is Your son."

At her words, Steve choked on a sob. "Thank you."

"I'm going to open the door now. Okay?" Marta said gently, holding her breath as she waited for his response.

He nodded, still crying, and she got up and walked towards the door on trembling legs. "It's me!" she called through the door to warn the policemen. "Steve is letting me out. He's not armed." She unbolted and opened the door to find two policemen ready to burst inside, as well as Angus and Paul in the hall behind them.

The police swiftly went in to arrest Steve, and Marta and Paul stared at each other, before she fell sobbing into his arms. He embraced her tightly, making soothing noises into her ear. Then he pressed his lips against hers. Angus smiled and looked away discreetly.

"I love you, Marta Rodriguez," Paul said, and there were tears in his eyes too. "But you're the most stubborn and willful woman I've ever met."

Marta laughed. "I love you, too," she said.

TWO DAYS LATER, Marta sat by Piper's bedside and watched her holding her son. Jack had been born by emergency C-section and, apart from being a few weeks early was in perfect health. Piper was sore but couldn't stop smiling, her eyes fixed on her baby. Despite the traumatic circumstances that had caused her to go into labour, Marta had hope that she would be fine. Steve had been taken away by the police and Marta knew he would be locked up, leaving Piper free to start a new life.

She had made enquiries about the refuge for Piper, but then her parents had turned up. Marta discovered that rather than them disowning their daughter as she'd been led to believe, it had been Piper who'd disappeared with Steve. Now they were reunited and standing by their daughter and grandson. Marta had been pleased to learn they were Christians, and as soon as they discovered who Marta was and heard about Angel, they started making plans for a visit. Both Piper and Marta wanted Angel and Jack to know each other since they were half-siblings.

Marta glanced at the clock. It was time to go. She kissed Piper and Jack goodbye and left the hospital to be met by Paul and Angel in his car. She got in the front passenger seat, smiling at her daughter and her boyfriend.

Although being attacked by Steve again had been traumatic, she found herself at an odd kind of peace. By helping to get Piper out of a disastrous situation and bring Steve to justice while also hopefully planting a seed for him that might one day lead him to the Lord, Marta felt like she had finally achieved some closure, and now she was free to move on with her life.

"Ready?" Paul asked.

Marta nodded and clipped in her seatbelt. They were on their way to pick up Maria to take her out for the afternoon. It would be the first time that she and Angel would meet each other, and Marta was nearly as excited as Angel was.

"Let's go," she said.

EPILOGUE

One year later

Marta held Paul's hand and stared into eyes brimming with love. How blessed she was to have this man promise to spend the rest of his life with her. Not in a million years could she have believed she would find a love so pure, so beautiful, so amazing. Unadulterated joy bubbled inside her and overflowed into the broad smile growing on her face.

The pastor cleared his throat. "You may now kiss the bride," he announced.

Paul cupped his hands around her face and gazed into her eyes before lowering his mouth towards hers. His lips pressed against hers, then gently covered her mouth. She quivered at the sweet tenderness of his kiss and couldn't wait until they were alone.

Only the enthusiastic clapping and whooping of the congregation caused them to draw apart.

Amy gave a huge whoop and Marta laughed.

They turned and walked down the aisle arm in arm, only to be showered in confetti.

Amy and Heidi walked behind her as bridesmaids, with Angel as flower girl and Archie as pageboy. Marta felt her heart would burst with joy. The past year had brought many changes and much fulfilment. She had carried on with her school talks and this had blossomed into a new career as a highly sought-after motivational speaker.

After what had happened with Steve, Paul had felt called to work with troubled adults and was now a prison chaplain. They both felt that they were in the vocations God wanted them to be in.

Steve had been arrested and charged and placed in a secure mental hospital. Marta was glad he was both out of harm's way and somewhere where he couldn't be a danger to anyone else.

She looked up to see Piper in the crowd, blowing her a kiss, her son on her hip. The two had struck up quite a friendship.

Maria was there, too, standing with Paul's family. They all looked overjoyed. Maria had quickly become a part of their lives and they saw her every second weekend and were planning on her moving in with them as she got older. She and Angel adored each other.

Marta looked at her new husband and said a silent prayer of gratitude for everything that God had brought into her life over the past year. Although she hadn't found a father, she had found Maria, and she had found Paul, who was the best father figure she could ask for to be there for Angel. As for her own father, although the situation was tragic, Marta had made her peace with her family's past.

She had her Heavenly Father, and that was more than enough.

This is His commandment, that we believe in the name of His Son Jesus Christ, and love one another, just as He commanded us. 1 John 3:23

A NOTE FROM THE AUTHOR

NOTE FROM THE AUTHOR

I hope you enjoyed "Because We Believed" and that it encouraged you in your walk with the Lord. If so, I'd truly appreciate you leaving a short review since reviews help others to find the book. It's my prayer that it will reach the hands of those who need to hear the message of hope that it contains.

Have you read the first three books in the series? If not, start with ebook *Because We Loved* for just 99c or read for free on KU. The books can all be read on their own, but you'll see familiar faces and God's transforming love in action in each of them.

To make sure you don't miss my next new release, why not join my Readers' list? You'll also receive a free thank-you copy of "Hank and Sarah - A Love Story", a clean love story with God at the center, simply for signing up.

Keep reading for a bonus chapter of "Her Kind-Hearted Billionaire". I think you'll enjoy it.

Blessings,
Juliette

Sydney, Australia

Nicholas Barrington sat behind his desk on the forty-fifth floor of the tower bearing his family's name and removed his pre-prepared meal from his lunch bag. Below, Sydney Harbour shimmered in the midday sun and looked spectacular. A small tugboat, looking much like a toy from this height, guided a large cruise ship through the harbour towards the heads, while a number of yachts sliced through the water easily in what Nick assumed was a strong breeze, given the trim of their sails. The problem was, being on the forty-fifth floor, he was removed from reality. The view was sensational, but he felt like a spectator. He'd much rather be a participant.

A firm knock sounded on his office door, pulling his gaze from the vista. Nicholas swivelled around. Alden, his brother and fellow director, sauntered in and sank into the chair on the opposite side of the desk. "Taking time for lunch today, bro?" At thirty-one, Alden was two years younger than Nicholas and had the same sea-blue eyes, although his hair was lighter.

"Yes. I was just about to eat. Did you bring yours?" For a

moment, Nicholas forgot he was talking with his brother. Of course Alden hadn't brought his lunch.

Alden scoffed, eyeing Nicholas's bag with amusement. "It'll be here in five minutes."

Nicholas pulled out his sandwich and salad, glad he didn't have to wait for his meal to be delivered.

"Eating in here today?" Charity, their younger sister, appeared in the doorway. The sharp bob framing her pixie-like face was the same dark colour as his, but she had their late mother's emerald green eyes. She plopped onto the chair next to Alden and pulled a portable blender filled with green powder from her carry bag. Opening a bottle of water, she poured half of it in and hit the button.

"That looks disgusting," Nicholas shouted over the whir of the machine.

"Try some if you like."

Grimacing, he quickly shook his head. "No thanks. I'll stick to my sandwich."

Moments later, a young man knocked tentatively on the door holding a rectangular food box. Alden waved him in and took the box.

Setting it on the desk, he peeled back the cardboard lid, revealing a large steak with new potatoes and green beans. Although it smelled appetising, as Nicholas took the last bite of his sandwich and moved onto the salad, he was thankful his tastes weren't the same as his siblings. He was a simple man with simple needs.

"It's all right, but it could be better," Alden commented after swallowing his first mouthful.

Nicholas ignored his brother's comment and instead

focused on Charity who'd just turned the blender off. The silence was very welcome.

"So, you know I was meant to be flying to Bali tomorrow for that meditation retreat?" Angling her head, she glanced at him as she poured some of the green concoction into a glass.

He nodded. Of late, Charity had been delving into meditation and something about self-praise and how to be her own deity. Not what Nicholas would have considered a worthwhile venture, but, each to his own. He'd started exploring things of a spiritual nature as well, but his initial explorations had led him to a traditional church, although he hadn't yet made up his mind whether that was what he wanted.

"Looks like I'll have to postpone the flight to another day." Charity released a frustrated sigh before taking a mouthful of what Nicholas considered a disgusting looking green concoction.

"Why's that?"

"Why?" Charity's green eyes bulged. "Because of that lazy pilot." Her voice rose to a crescendo and Nicholas wouldn't have been surprised if the whole floor had heard.

"Ugh, don't even get me started." Alden shook his head, waving a fork in the air.

Charity leaned forward. "Can you believe he told me he can't work tomorrow? I mean, I'm his boss. It's not like we're ordering him to fly every day. He gets plenty of time off. I just needed him for one day."

"Why can't he take you?" Nicholas asked in a calm voice.

"His daughter's having surgery. I get that family is important and all that, but honestly, it's only a few hours each way. He'd be back before she even woke up."

Nicholas studied his sister with sadness. He doubted she knew that Roger's small daughter had been born with special needs and her surgeries required extensive preparation. Even the anesthesia was a risk. But it was no use saying anything. She wouldn't understand or care. "Did he suggest anyone else who could step in?"

"I don't want anyone else. They wouldn't know our plane like he does." Charity blew out another breath and sipped her concoction. "Anyway, I think we should fire him." Shifting in her chair, she crossed her long, slim legs and adjusted her skirt.

"I agree," Alden said. "Last time he took me to Dubai, we were an hour late. He said it was because they didn't have a place for us to land, but isn't it his job to make sure all of that's figured out ahead of time?"

Nicholas sighed. "That's hardly his fault. Sometimes unexpected things happen that are out of anyone's control. You know Roger's competent and he always does his best."

"You're so naive, big brother. You always want to see the good in everybody. No wonder they take advantage of you." Alden gave him a withering look.

Nicholas pursed his lips. He wished his siblings could show a little more humility and understanding, especially since they'd been given so much. How could they be so cruel and selfish when it came to others?

Taking a sip from his water bottle, Nicholas shut out his siblings as they continued talking about things he couldn't relate to. Although the three were very different, it saddened him they weren't closer. Without any other family, they only had each other. But all they ever talked about was the business and what gave them pleasure, like Charity's Bali trip.

Beyond that, very little of depth ever entered their conversations. While the two continued to talk about things of no interest to him, Nicholas returned to his work, but his ears pricked when Alden mentioned their late grandfather, James Barrington.

"You know, old James wouldn't have liked us wasting the money on a lousy staffer. Just because a man's nice enough doesn't make him worth the money." It seemed they'd returned to the issue of whether to fire Roger or not. Nicholas groaned. From what he remembered of James Barrington, firing a man because of an important family issue would have been the last thing he would have done.

When he died, the three siblings had inherited their grandfather's fortune, amassed during the mining boom of the eighties. A billion for each, plus the company divided between them. Now the trio lacked for nothing, but as much as Nicholas appreciated the life he now had, he would much have preferred his grandfather, and his parents, to still be alive. How different things would have been if his parents had inherited instead of the three grandchildren.

He sighed sadly. Yes, he'd give just about anything to have his parents back. It didn't seem fair that their lives had been snuffed out while they were still in their prime.

"So, do you think we should fire him? After he takes me to Bali, of course?" Charity asked nonchalantly, inspecting her perfectly manicured nails.

"Don't be a fool," Alden said harshly.

For a moment, Nicholas held hopes that his brother might stick up for the man, but they were soon dashed when Alden continued. "You should probably wait until he brings you back from Bali. You don't want to be stuck there!" He laughed, and Charity joined in.

Nicholas seethed. He had to say something, but he needed to remain calm and rational. An emotional defense of the pilot wouldn't go over well with his siblings. "Why don't we give him another chance? His daughter is having surgery, it's hardly a time to be selfish."

Charity huffed with exasperation. "Whatever you say, big brother. Although I don't see how it affects you, since you never use the private jet, anyway." Her voice dripped with sarcasm.

Biting his lip, Nicholas brushed her comments and attitude off. They'd soon forget about the pilot and move on to a discussion about shoes or something as equally trivial.

"Well, I'm headed out. I've got a hot yoga class this afternoon." Charity stood, tossed her rubbish in the bin, and then picked up her blender.

"Don't you need more than that shake before working out?" Alden waved the last piece of steak on his fork as if he were teasing her with it.

She rolled her eyes. "Keep your cow, thanks." With that, she turned and left the room, teetering on her stilettos.

Alden mopped up the last of his gravy, said a brief goodbye to Nicholas, and then also left the office.

Leaning back in his chair, Nicholas released a slow breath and gazed out the window. The cruise ship was long gone, but a Manly ferry was approaching Circular Quay, leaving white frothy water in its wake.

As much as he loved his siblings, he also loved his peace and quiet. He sometimes wondered about their grandfather and whether he'd be pleased with how his grandchildren were handling his fortune. James Barrington was renowned for his kindness, a rarity in the ruthless mining industry, and Nicholas wished he'd gotten to know him better before he passed. He sensed he could have learned a lot from him, and not just about the business. He'd heard that James Barrington was a religious man. Another rarity in the industry.

Swivelling his chair all the way around, Nicholas set back to work, tapping his fingers on the keyboard, opening emails from clients, studying spreadsheets. Millions of dollars in transactions and exchanges occurred on a weekly basis and the company was doing well, but as Managing Director, he needed to stay on top of it.

Their clients were happy, and he had reason to be proud of the company that he and his siblings had maintained and grown since taking over almost ten years ago. To the world at large, they were a success.

But sometimes, in the still of night, when he had time to think, he pondered what success really was. What was he missing by spending all his days on the forty-fifth floor?

Grab Her Kind-Hearted Billionaire to continue reading.

OTHER BOOKS BY JULIETTE DUNCAN

Find all of Juliette Duncan's books on her website:
www.julietteduncan.com/library

Billionaires with Heart Christian Romance Series

Her Kind-Hearted Billionaire

A reluctant billionaire, a grieving young woman, and the trip that changes their lives forever...

Her Generous Billionaire

A grieving billionaire, a solo mother, and a woman determined to sabotage their relationship...

Her Disgraced Billionaire

A billionaire in jail, a nurse who cares, and the challenge that changes their lives forever...

"The Billionaires with Heart Christian Romance Series" is a series of stand-alone books that are both God honoring and entertaining. Get your copy now, enjoy and be blessed!

A Time for Everything Series

A Time For Everything Series is a mature-age contemporary Christian romance series set in Sydney, Australia and Texas, USA. If you like real-life characters, faith-filled families, and friendships that become something more, then you'll love these inspirational second-chance romances.

Transformed by Love Christian Romance Series

Book 1 - *Because We Loved*

A decorated Lieutenant Colonel plagued with guilt. A captivating widow whose husband was killed under his watch…

Book 2 - *Because We Forgave*

A fallen TV personality hiding from his failures. An ex-wife and family facing their fears…

Book 3 - *Because We Dreamed*

When dreams are shattered, can hope be restored?

Book 4 - *Because We Believed*

A young woman seeking her family. A young man searching for love...

The True Love Series

Set in Australia, what starts out as simple love story grows into a family saga, including a dad battling bouts of depression and guilt, an ex-wife with issues of her own, and a young step-mum trying to mother a teenager who's confused and hurting. Through it all, a love story is woven. A love story between a caring God and His precious children as He gently draws them to Himself and walks with them through the trials and joys of life.

"A beautiful Christian story. I enjoyed all of the books in this series. They all brought out Christian concepts of faith in action."

"Wonderful set of books. Weaving the books from story to story. Family living, God, & learning to trust Him with all their hearts."

The Precious Love Series

The Precious Love Series continues the story of Ben, Tessa and Jayden from the The True Love Series, although each book can be read on its own. All of the books in this series will warm your heart and draw you closer to the God who loves and cherishes you without condition.

"I loved all the books by Juliette, but those about Jaydon and Angie's stories are my favorites...can't wait for the next one..."

"Juliette Duncan has earned my highest respect as a Christian romance writer. She continues to write such touching stories about real life and the tragedies, turmoils, and joys that happen while we are living. The words that she uses to write about her characters relationships with God can only come from someone that has had a very close & special with her Lord and Savior herself. I have read all of her books and if you are a reader of Christian fiction books I would highly recommend her books." Vicki

The Shadows Series

An inspirational romance, a story of passion and love, and of God's

inexplicable desire to free people from pasts that haunt them so they can live a life full of His peace, love and forgiveness, regardless of the circumstances. Book 1, *"Lingering Shadows"* is set in England, and follows the story of Lizzy, a headstrong, impulsive young lady from a privileged background, and Daniel, a roguish Irishman who sweeps her off her feet. But can Lizzy leave the shadows of her past behind and give Daniel the love he deserves, and will Daniel find freedom and release in God?

Hank and Sarah - A Love Story, *the Prequel to "The Madeleine Richards Series" is a FREE thank you gift for joining my mailing list. You'll also be the first to hear about my next books and get exclusive sneak previews. Get your free copy at www.julietteduncan.com/subscribe*

The Madeleine Richards Series

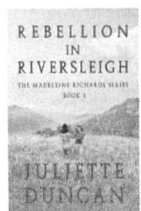

Although the 3 book series is intended mainly for pre-teen/ Middle Grade girls, it's been read and enjoyed by people of all ages.

"Juliette has a fabulous way of bringing her characters to life. Maddy is at typical teenager with authentic views and actions that truly make it feel like you are feeling her pain and angst. You want to enter into her situation and make everything better. Mom and soon to be dad respond to her with love and gentle persuasion while maintaining their faith and trust in Jesus, whom they know, will give them wisdom as they continue on their lives journey. Appropriate for teenage readers but any age can enjoy." Amazon Reader

The Potter's House Books...stories of hope, redemption, and second chances. Find out more here:

http://pottershousebooks.com/our-books/

The Homecoming
Can she surrender a life of fame and fortune to find true love?

Unchained
Imprisoned by greed – redeemed by love

Blessings of Love

She's going on mission to help others. He's going to win her heart.

The Hope We Share

Can the Master Potter work in Rachel and Andrew's hearts and give them a second chance at love?

Stand Alone Christian Romantic Suspense

Leave Before He Kills You

When his face grew angry, I knew he could murder...

That face drove me and my three young daughters to flee across Australia.

I doubted he'd ever touch the girls, but if I wanted to live and see them grow, I had to do something.

The plan my friend had proposed was daring and bold, but it also gave me hope.

My heart thumped. What if he followed?

Radical, honest and real, this Christian romantic suspense is one woman's journey to freedom you won't put down…get your copy and read it now.

ABOUT THE AUTHOR

Juliette Duncan is a Christian fiction author, passionate about writing stories that will touch her readers' hearts and make a difference in their lives. Although a trained school teacher, Juliette spent many years working alongside her husband in their own business, but is now relishing the opportunity to follow her passion for writing stories she herself would love to read. Based in Brisbane, Australia, Juliette and her husband have five adult children, eight grandchildren, and an elderly long haired dachshund. Apart from writing, Juliette loves exploring the great world we live in, and has travelled extensively, both within Australia and overseas. She also enjoys social dancing and eating out.

Connect with Juliette:

Email: juliette@julietteduncan.com

Website: www.julietteduncan.com

Facebook: www.facebook.com/JulietteDuncanAuthor

Twitter: https://twitter.com/Juliette_Duncan

Printed in Great Britain
by Amazon